SUDDEN FEAR

BARTLETT BROTHERS
SUDDEN FEAR
ROGER ELWOOD

WORD
Kids!

WORD PUBLISHING
Dallas · London · Vancouver · Melbourne

SUDDEN FEAR

Copyright © 1991 by Roger Elwood.

Scripture quotations are from *International Children's Bible, New Century Version,* copyright © 1983, 1986, 1988 by Word Publishing, Dallas, Texas 75039.

Library of Congress Cataloging-in-Publication Data

Elwood, Roger.
    Sudden fear / Roger Elwood.
       p. cm.—(The Bartlett brothers)
    "Word Kids!"
    Summary: The teenage sons of an American diplomat find their lives in danger when they intercept a terrorist's message.
    ISBN 0–8499–3301–3
    [1. Brothers—Fiction. 2. Terrorism—Fiction. 3. Adventure and adventurers—Fiction.] I. Title. II. Series: Elwood, Roger. Bartlett brothers.
PZ7. E554Su 1991
[Fic]—dc20   91–13847
                                        CIP
                                          AC

Printed in the United States of America

1 2 3 4 5 6 9 RRD 9 8 7 6 5 4 3 2 1

To
John Long
For believing in me

 **One**

Fourteen-year-old Ryan Bartlett adjusted his metal-rimmed glasses as he looked up from the flickering images on his computer screen. He was puzzled over what he had been reading for the past few seconds.

PLAN GOING WELL. . . .

Letter by letter words unexpectedly had begun to appear onscreen as typed through a remote connection with some distant and unknown computer user.

Again! he thought, eager to see all of the message that he suspected only he knew had been somehow intercepted.

For a while it seemed as though the cause of these kinds of accidental interceptions had been taken care of, that all that phone company wiring actually *had* been fixed. At least, that was what some script-reading company spokesman had stated during one of the evening television news programs.

1

Yet Ryan was learning soon enough to take public announcements like that with a grain of salt, chalking these up more to public relations, not to any attempt at corporate honesty.

Wiring somewhere in the system, someone too anxious to finish working for the day and not paying attention. . . .

Ryan was certain that this was the cause of his present dilemma, and he fully expected the phone company to give him some sort of double talk when he reported it.

More! There was more on screen, more of the message.

PLAN GOING WELL. TAKEOVER IMMINENT. . . .

Nothing special there, really. And yet–

EVERYTHING FALLING INTO PLACE. ALLAH WILL BE PLEASED.

Ryan realized something that made him nervous, something that grabbed at him so that it seemed like a physical thing rather than being purely in his mind.

The message was continuing!

It hadn't been cut off as quickly as it had appeared.

Unlike in those previous situations when somehow the unintended connection ended almost as soon as—.

Different. It wasn't stopping! It—!

My hands! he thought as he looked at them in

surprise. *They're—!*

His palms were sweaty, though he had no idea why this was the case in view of what seemed, at that early stage, to be harmless enough, nothing special to make him feel the way he did. Only his guilt over having stayed with it so long was justified!

Allah . . . the Muslim name for God.

Ryan wondered if whoever it was at the opposite end was in the Middle East at that very moment.

That would be something, he told himself. He'd never had an interception from outside the United States.

But *Allah?* Now that was really a whole other kind of message, definitely more mysterious than any he'd ever seen.

Ryan had studied enough of the history of Islam, the religion of Muslims, to be thankful for his own Christian faith.

Just think! What if I had been born in Iraq or Syria or some place like that, and been raised as a—?

It was one more aspect of his life to be grateful for, one more reason to thank God for having had the kind of parents he had been blessed with over the years. And he knew that his brother Chad felt exactly the same way.

But, here, today, it was another matter of a

different nature that he had to tackle—his homework.

I can't use the computer while they're on line. . . .

Ryan's patience was never very durable, and he was beginning to run out of it.

"Get out of my space," he shouted, knowing, of course, that the other guy couldn't hear. "Get out of my space, whoever you are!"

He knew he could turn off the computer and start over again, but it was a complicated hassle he didn't need just then. So he sat back as calmly as he could, drumming his fingers on top of the desk. Computers! Sometimes, the frustration level was high enough that he almost gave up on them altogether. There were mechanical reasons, such as parts that stopped working, then started working again just as the repairman arrived. But there were other reasons, too, including the time he accidentally intercepted a message designed to steal another guy's girlfriend.

"WHADDAYA WANT WITH FOUR-EYES? HE LOOKS LIKE A WORM WITH GLASSES ON—YEAH, A BOOKWORM!"

Ryan's left hand went instinctively to his own glasses as he remembered that message. He had really been upset over that one.

"Oh, well," he sighed, but stopped short as he reread the latest message on his screen. The next-to-the-last word had set off some sort of inner alarm.

Takeover.

He had repeated it again and again in his mind over the past quarter hour or so. But now something was beginning to tumble into place the longer he focused on it and the rest of the message.

"Uh, huh. . . ." he muttered.

Takeover.

He had been ready to disregard that word but now held on, not quite knowing why. In fact, he wasn't sure of very much, least of all the way he was responding.

What *could* it mean? Had he somehow linked in with a transmission from a moneyman at one of the major stockbroker firms?

Something made Ryan hang on just a bit longer without simply switching to another program or turning off the computer and going into the kitchen to get something to eat. He seemed to remember a first-class, stuffed-full-of-goodies submarine sandwich just waiting for him—that is, if his always starved brother Chad hadn't gotten there ahead of him. It would be the first time this would have happened!

Chad gets so frustrated, poor guy, Ryan was thinking. *He can eat a couple of candy bars and put on five pounds. Then he tries to compensate by working out to get it off. But I can eat almost a truckload of jelly donuts and raisin cookies plus a quart of ice cream and not gain more than a few ounces.*

Ryan ended up hardly moving at all, let alone toward the refrigerator, his attention held by the 16-inch screen in front of him. He knew the word *takeover* could also have a more brutal meaning, the takeover of an entire country, often with violent results.

Could that be it? he wondered.

Somehow there was an uneasiness beginning in his stomach, something that stayed with him.

Ridiculous! So ridiculous! he thought. This out-of-the-blue electronic note was probably from some unknown guy, or maybe it was a girl saying nothing that they meant to be sinister in any way. He figured if he knew what it was really all about, he would feel very, very foolish.

And yet, he couldn't get around the fact that it *felt* somehow odd. *Real* odd—as in dangerous.

His gaze locked in on the screen after drifting away for a moment or two.

Blank.

He waited a few seconds, but there was nothing else at that point.

That's the end of it, he thought, breathing a sigh of relief, the submarine sandwich back in his thoughts.

He switched to something else and started typing another access code. Suddenly the screen was no longer blank. But for very much the wrong reason.

N-o! his mind shouted. *No, that just can't be. It can't!*

Another message or else more of the same one started to appear on the monitor.

WE MUST TRY NOT TO DISPOSE OF ANYONE . . . AT LEAST AT THE BEGINNING. LATER WILL BE THE BEST TIME FOR THAT SORT OF THING.

Ryan's throat muscles tightened as he repeated just one word—*dispose* . . . as in kill?

Ryan swallowed with difficulty a couple of times, hoping that the message would end right there, that the jokester or whoever would grow tired and—

"That's not cool, not cool at all," he said, disgusted with whoever was at the other end of the computer network. "Playing around like that is not funny."

The impact of what he suspected might be happening hit him hard.

Fear. . . .

Fear that everything was running like sand between his fingers, and he'd never be able to get back any of it.

Sudden fear, ugly fear that—

Ryan abrubtly pushed himself back from his desk, the rollers on his chair squeaking a bit.

That final sentence repeated itself in his mind, like the chilling letters on the monitor itself.

Later will be the best time. . . .

He swallowed hard.

. . . for that sort of thing.

Ryan felt completely alone. It was as though he had gotten a secret announcement about the end of the world, and nobody else was around to tell.

Perspiration spread from his palms and back over the rest of his body as he thought of two words that seemed to complete what the other computer user intended to say all along.

Later will be the best time . . . FOR MURDER!

Ryan sat still only for a second or two longer.

"Chad!" he said as he jumped to his feet.

His heart pounding, he raced down the hallway to his brother's bedroom. Empty. Chad had left.

Of course! Wrestling practice is on Thursday afternoons, he thought. *Chad went back to school after driving me home.*

He headed for a phone in the hallway, picked up the receiver, and started to dial the police but stopped before he got to the last number.

No! Be calm. Think, think, think, will ya? It may not be anything for the police to deal with.

Ryan slammed the receiver down. He was thinking more clearly now.

Dad's taught us to look at everything and pick it apart piece-by-piece, he reminded himself. *Don't fly off the handle. The other guy never said murder. It's what you added in your own mind. Stop trying to anticipate the thoughts of someone you've never met. There could be a dozen explanations for that message.*

But what did they mean by "dispose of"? Maybe it was just the purchase of a big corporation, and some employees were going to lose their jobs.

He started laughing out loud.

Listen to that stuff inside your head, Ryan, he told himself. *Lots of jumpin'-the-gun garbage in there. Slow down that overactive imagination of yours and get a hold of yourself.*

Standing there in the hallway, he was feeling more and more foolish. He was glad that he had not gone ahead with that phone call, especially when he imagined what fun they would make of him at police headquarters. He could almost hear them: *"One of Andrew Bartlett's kids has gone bonkers!"* When your dad is a special envoy of the U.S. State Department everyone seems to know him!

Ryan didn't have to *be* there to see Sergeant Gavin Mulrooney having a rip-snorting field day with that sort of stuff. After all, he was sure Sergeant Mulrooney remembered their previous encounter . . . the time Ryan overheard a kidnapping plot through fancy hidden microphones he had assembled himself.

Unfortunately, Sergeant Mulrooney had thought that Ryan was just another crazy kid engaged in some kind of practical joke. And Ryan was never

able to convince him otherwise nor to help whoever was being kidnapped.

Will Sergeant Mulrooney ever take me seriously?
Ryan wondered.

Then he relaxed a bit, sighing.

*Maybe that's one advantage of getting older.
Someday I won't react as crazy as this.*

He started chuckling, thankful that Chad
wasn't home just then to witness the rise and fall
of a teenage computer junkie. Then he slapped
his forehead with the palm of his left hand.

"Dummy! The computer! You forgot to turn it
off . . ."

He headed back to his room, now whistling as
he entered.

"Whoa!" he gasped.

There was more stuff on the monitor.

STOP TRANSMITTING. SOMEONE'S—

Ryan froze in the middle of the floor, his eyes
locked in on what was now showing up on screen.

Someone's—

His mind filled in the rest of the words almost
without having to read them.

. . . been "listening" in. Someone knows!

Ryan sat down again at the desk, clearing the
screen. From some neglected corner of his mind,
he was remembering something . . . . His father
had become a member of some kind of diplomatic
news service.

"Where's that access code?" he asked out loud, annoyed that when he needed to be better organized, he actually wasn't. "Where—?"

After leafing through a folder of odds-and-ends of paper, he found the code and typed it into the computer, thinking of Andrew Bartlett as he did so.

His dad was somewhere in the Middle East now. Not even Ryan knew the specific place. Government rules and regulations were strict: Family members could be told nothing that would violate the secrecy that surrounded virtually every mission. But Ryan and his brother knew their dad was much more than a distinguished special envoy in the U.S. State Department. And each time he left their Southern California home on one of his missions, the three of them prayed together for protection and safety. They always kept a spot in their wood-panelled family room for Mom who could never join them again, but still that opening in the circle was there, out of habit or whatever.

Mom . . . miss you, he thought. *Miss you very much.*

The computer was beeping. It did that each time a program newly appeared on screen.

Ryan scrolled through item after item:

News about oil prices; a coup in one of the African nations; a report about guerrilla activity in the Philippines; Israeli intelligence reporting—.

He stopped scrolling, locking in on that last item.

Israeli intelligence warns of forthcoming terrorist attacks . . . his heart was suddenly beating faster, . . . in the United States. Muslim radicals will try a takeover of—.

Takeover . . . there it was again! He almost didn't see the rest of the message.

That one part hit him hard enough that it seemed physical—and a staggering blow at that. A feeling of sickness was taking over every inch of his stomach.

His mind flashed back to the message he had intercepted earlier, *"Plan going well. Takeover imminent."*

And now this latest bit of information, this time from a reliable source!

His eyes refocused on the monitor, and the rest of that news service message

—of Washington, D.C.!

Ryan felt a dull ache grip his head, six earlier words repeating themselves in his mind, words he wished he hadn't ever seen.

Someone's been listening in. Someone knows!

 # Two

Arm and leg muscles tired, neck aching from a hold his opponent had locked onto him, Chad Bartlett was heading for the shower stalls adjacent to his high school's gymnasium. He looked forward to the hot needle-point jets of water massaging some of the pain away.

"Hold up, Bartlett!"

The familiar voice of his wrestling coach stopped him.

"Yes, Mr. Williamson," he said, hoping that whatever it was wouldn't take long.

"Emergency call," the tall and stocky middle-aged man told him. "Your brother. Use my office phone."

Not again, Ryan!

Sweaty and irritable, Chad turned around and walked back across the gym toward the coach's office.

This better be good!

He managed to find the phone after searching for it on a battered old desk that looked like a dump site for everything *but* toxic wastes.

"Yeah, Ryan, what's going down?" the sixteen-year-old asked.

Chad listened as his younger brother told him what had happened.

"Is *that* what you're excited about?" Chad said finally. "Man, Dad's in the spy business, not us."

He turned his head, instantly realizing his carelessness and hoping that no one had heard him.

What a dummy, he told himself. *You gotta be more careful than that, stupid.*

Fortunately the coach was busy talking to another wrestler in the gym; otherwise Chad was alone.

He breathed a sigh of relief.

"Yeah, I know, real dumb," he had to admit when Ryan scolded him. "But not as dumb as your getting yourself all worked up over some clever practical joker playing around with his computer."

Ryan was asking him to come home right away.

"Where's Miss Stephenson?" he asked. She was the housekeeper their dad had hired to fix meals and generally watch after them. Mostly, she let Chad and Ryan do as they wished, and they liked her pretty well. Of course, she wasn't, as no one could be, a substitute for their mother.

"She's at the store. She thinks we'll starve if she doesn't have a month's supply of food in the pantry! So come on home, will ya?"

Chad hesitated. Though Ryan was two years younger, he wasn't a little kid anymore. The demands and pressures of being the sons of a veteran secret agent had brought both of them closer to being adults faster than many other guys their ages. Almost every day they had some adult-size decisions to make.

Besides, Ryan had proven so intelligent that he had already become a high school sophomore, leapfrogging over scores of former classmates by skipping the first year. This tended to cause arguments between Ryan and him, arguments grounded in some jealousy on Chad's part.

My brother, the brain, Chad thought. *But I love the little guy, anyway.*

There had been times when he needed to come to Ryan's rescue. Short eggheads were easy targets for burly school bullies. It was a little easier for Chad to help out since he was at least as strong and as tough as any other student might be, except an actual giant of a guy. But the only giants he knew were nice and gentle, interested only in sports and not in beating up kid brothers.

"My brawn saves your brain yet again," Chad had told Ryan after one encounter.

15

"That guy *needed* a few less teeth," Ryan had said as he stood, wobbling a bit and brushing off the gravel from his clothes.

Chad was smiling at that one when he realized his brother was still on the other end of the phone line.

"Okay, okay," he said finally. "Just give me a few minutes, will you?"

They both were about to hang up when Chad added, impulsively, "It'll be all right, Ryan. It always is, you know."

After leaving the coach's office, he headed for the showers again, realizing that what he said last was wrong. Actually everything didn't always turn out right. No matter how hard they hoped and prayed, some things went the opposite of what they wanted.

Mom. . . .

She had been taken from them three years earlier, killed when the family car exploded.

The very hardest thing was standing by her coffin and saying good-bye for the last time.

Ryan, only eleven years old at the time, had bent down and kissed her on the forehead, then pulled back suddenly.

"What's wrong?" Chad had whispered.

"It's so cold!" his brother had said, tears rolling down his cheeks.

"Naturally," Chad had told him a little sharply, then hesitated, and added, "Mom's not there, you know."

"I do, Chad, I do know. But . . . but—."

"But what?"

"Dad's into some stuff, you know, and . . . and what if—?"

Chad had reached out and hugged his brother, and somehow they and Andrew Bartlett had made it through the sad days, weeks, and even months that followed. At one point early on, Chad had approached his father, when Ryan wasn't around, and put a question to him that he couldn't admit in front of his little brother.

"*Why*, Dad?" Chad asked his father. "What happened?"

Andrew Bartlett could never tell him then or later the full story. Some details were restricted under a TOP SECRET heading for the sake of national security. And it was strictly forbidden to reveal anything labeled in this manner.

National security! Chad had mentally sneered more than once. *What about our security as a family?* he thought. *Where was it when Mom—?*

"It has to do with my job," Mr. Bartlett said simply, interrupting Chad's thoughts.

"Your job?" Chad countered. "Dad, are you telling me that your job was somehow behind Mom's murder?"

Andrew Bartlett looked at his son, knowing, of course, that he could lie. There seemed little or no chance that Chad would ever find out the truth.

17

But he also realized that he had taught his sons to detest lying, to avoid it altogether. And he wouldn't lie himself, no matter how hard the truth would be for Chad to have to cope with just then.

"Yes, son, yes, it was."

"Then quit the job, Dad," Chad pleaded. "Get into something else. First, it was Mom. Maybe next it'll be you . . . or us."

Mr. Bartlett winced at that.

"I do what I do, Chad, in order to help my country, to preserve freedom and—."

"Oh stop it, Dad," Chad interrupted him, his cheeks red with the emotion of anger, deep anger. "I've heard speeches like that before. I'm tired of them. So was Mom."

Though Mr. and Mrs. Bartlett were close and loving parents, he could see how much pressure his father's work had caused. Many times his mother would go to bed crying, and, through the closed bedroom door, he had heard her praying for strength and wisdom.

"You're away more than you are home," Chad said. "Ryan and I never know when a phone call will tell us that you've been taken hostage or murdered."

How much they yearned to have him there with them! How many times Ryan and he would sit and watch scratchy home movies or slides of the family together! Flickering images became a desperate substitute for the real thing.

Father and son had been sitting in two folding chairs in the large backyard area of the two-story house they had shared as a family for nearly a dozen years.

Chad looked straight into his father's eyes.

"*Mom* wanted you to quit, too. She hated the danger you—."

He cut himself off, bowing his head.

"What is it, Chad?" Mr. Bartlett asked, deeply concerned.

Still looking down at his lap, Chad put a question to his father that had been bothering him for a long time.

"Did you ever wonder if maybe you were the target, Dad? Maybe Mom was murdered by mistake."

Mr. Bartlett stood then, a bit unsteadily, his back to his son.

Chad raised his head. "Dad?" he asked.

"I heard you, son, I heard."

Chad was quiet. He could see that his father was going through some kind of struggle. Apparently his question had been right on target.

"Yes, Chad, I've thought about it," Andrew Bartlett said, his voice not much above a whisper. He turned to face his son, tears streaming down his cheeks. "It's a burden that I've had to put before the Lord again and again, and ask His help with it, begging Him to take it off my shoulders."

Seeing his father break down in front of him like that helped Chad realize that sharing grief was important. Bearing it alone was the worst thing that any of them could do.

Chad stood, hugged his dad, and the two of them, father and son, smiled through their tears.

"We'll make it, Dad, we will," Chad said, hoping he sounded more convincing than he felt. "You know that 'God works for the good of those who love Him.'"

It was easy for Chad to quote from the Bible. He and his brother had been taught early on to memorize a few helpful verses and keep them handy for moments like that.

But Chad knew that God's Word wasn't a collection of little magic wands that could be waved around in the air and everything would be okay.

He had discovered that fact soon enough, when the pain was still there and his mother's body remained in its grave. It was *not* some awful midnight dream from which he would awaken to find that it wasn't true. She was really gone.

Years later, there were moments—sometimes when he was asleep, sometimes when he was awake—that he just couldn't get out of his mind. In one of these, he would be inside the house looking for his mother, calling out to her. Then she would yell to him from the garden out back. He would run through the house and into the yard, and there she would be, bending down, her hands dirty, a bandana around her hair, a bright smile on her face.

Oh, Mom, Chad said, though not out loud. He was getting dressed after his shower, his well-defined muscles feeling better now. *We miss you—we miss you a lot, in so many ways.*

He paused, his shirt hanging from one shoulder.

He missed *hearing* that familiar voice telling Ryan and him that breakfast was ready, and they'd better hurry before it got cold. He missed *smelling* the odor of bacon cooking and, sometimes, the extra treat of freshly baked bread in the oven.

He missed *seeing* their mother and father sitting together on those days they weren't separated by thousands of miles.

It's simple stuff, Mom, stuff that happened every morning of our lives. And all of us took it for granted until, one day, we couldn't hear you or see you anymore.

Chad wiped his eyes with the back of his hand.

Remembering hurt.

Two hundred miles away, two young men sat in front of a computer monitor.

They were linked in with a network of computers in Washington, D.C., and half a dozen other

American cities as well as the central command post in Baghdad, Iraq.

WE DO NOT KNOW HOW IT COULD HAVE HAPPENED.

The one named Mohammed had typed those words.

The next response came from a secret location in the Iraqi capital. It was immediate and terse.

NO EXCUSES CAN BE ALLOWED. YOU WERE SUPPOSED TO BE ON A CODED FREQUENCY. YOU TRIPPED UP. SUCH MISTAKES CAN BE DEADLY.

Mohammed, frustrated and scared, typed: WHAT IS THE NEXT STEP?

Instantly, from more than 10,000 miles away: WE HAVE STORED RECORDS OF ALL TRANSMISSIONS TO AND FROM YOUR LOCATION. OUR ADVANCED PROGRAMMING WILL TRACE ALMOST EVERYTHING. FIRST, WE FIND THE GENERAL LOCATION, AND THEN LOCK IN ON THE EXACT SPOT WHEN THERE IS ANOTHER TRANSMISSION FROM IT.

New computer developments now provided for tracing of electronic messages in a manner not unlike what was involved in tracing phone calls. Mohammed didn't understand the technology, but he appreciated the fact that it existed.

The message from headquarters concluded with: ONCE WE FIND OUT WHO IS INVOLVED, YOU MUST ELIMINATE THE INTERCEPTOR. IS THAT UNDERSTOOD?

Mohammed signed off by typing: IT IS. WE DO OUR BEST.

He turned to his friend named Ishtar. "How can we find a needle in a haywire, as the Americans call it?" he asked, obviously nervous.

"*Haystack*, Mohammed," Ishtar corrected him, chuckling a bit as he did so.

"Whatever it happens to be," the other replied, grunting. "I mean, how do we do this?"

"We send a phony message," Ishtar remarked. "We hope the Americans, whoever they are, take the bait."

"But what if it was a . . . a fluke . . . and never happens again?"

"Then we have nothing to worry about, do we?"

Mohammed leaned back in his chair, rubbing his chin, feeling very tired and nervous.

"I hope that you are correct," he said. "We must never displease our leader, you know that."

Ishtar nodded, for he knew all too well. Two missing fingers were evidence of that.

 **Three**

Ryan jumped at every phone call and every other sound, including the front door bell ringing.

A parcel delivery service had just left a package addressed to his father. He thanked the deliveryman, and then shut the door quickly and locked it again.

The package was only about ten by five by four inches. Ryan carried it to his father's den and put it on top of his desk.

Then he hurried back to the computer. Nothing else alarming had showed up in the twenty minutes since he had spoken to Chad. But he had spent some more time with that diplomatic news service and was astonished to find Andrew Bartlett's name mentioned.

SPECIAL ENVOY ANDREW BARTLETT IS CURRENTLY IN SYRIA. . . .

Ryan gulped a couple of times. Syria was a country noted for its support of international terrorism.

But its leaders had recently turned toward the West as the result of the war with Iraq in the Middle East.

"Dad, what in the world are you doing there?" Ryan voiced the first question that came to mind.

Apparently someone at the news service must have been thinking along the same lines.

ONE WONDERS IF HIS MISSION IS TIED IN WITH THE RECENT MUSLIM THREATS AGAINST TARGETS IN THE UNITED STATES.

What kind of coincidence was that?

Just half an hour earlier, Ryan had intercepted words which seemed to suggest something that might tie in with—.

A loud sound interrupted his thoughts.

That must be Chad!

Ryan thought he had heard his brother's car pull up in the driveway. The special mufflers Chad had installed himself always announced his arrival unmistakably. Chad seemed to alternate between working on the car or his big, black, chrome-edged Harley that was an equal pride and joy.

Ryan envied his brother's mechanical skills.

He stood and started toward the front door, hesitating a second or two as he listened. The sound was different. It wasn't Chad.

Once again Ryan started to sweat as he walked down the hallway, then through the living room to the entry way.

He cautiously pulled back a curtain to look outside.

Nothing. No car. No truck.

Wait a minute! It's coming from above.

He opened the door and walked out onto the front porch, peeking up from under the sloping roof. A helicopter. A very loud helicopter was circling the neighborhood.

Ryan ducked back, then instantly felt foolish again, realizing that he was making himself a nervous wreck.

The helicopter seemed to be veering away just as Chad's car entered the street.

In a couple of seconds, his brother had made it to the driveway.

The pilot's hesitating. He's—!

That did seem to be the case, as though he were surveying the car, but then the helicopter flew off very quickly.

Chad was standing in the driveway, looking up and scratching his head as Ryan rushed out to him.

"Did you see that?" he asked excitedly.

"Yeah, I did," Chad replied. "A helicopter. So what? I admit it caught me a little by surprise but that's all."

"Didn't it seem strange?"

"What *are* you talking about, Ryan? We've had birds like that fly over us before. No big deal."

"But—but—the—the—," Ryan started, then stopped himself.

He looked sheepish all of a sudden, realizing how dumb he must have seemed to Chad.

"I guess you're right. I'm overreacting."

"Bingo!" Chad said.

In the house, Ryan went through everything again with his brother, adding the latest bit of information from the news service.

"There's *nothing* to connect Dad with what you picked up," Chad said, annoyed and frustrated that his brother didn't have common sense along with that extra brain power. "Don't you see that, Ryan? This thing's gotten hold of you, and I just don't know why."

"But—."

"But nothing, Ryan. This was silly before, when you called me at the gym. But it's getting to be *worse* the more I think about it."

Chad stood abruptly, the irritation he felt showing in his body language.

"I'm going back to the school to watch some tapes from my last match," he said. "I don't have time to waste like you do."

Ryan was on his feet as well, his face red, not with anger but real anxiety.

"Please, Chad, please do this for me. I have a feeling about this. I can't explain it better than that. Maybe it's that still small voice Dad keeps telling us to listen to whenever it's trying to tell us something."

Chad was hesitating, halfway wanting to turn and go, leaving Ryan to stew in his silliness.

"I've *got* to show you the printout. Skim it for me, Chad. Please . . . that's all I ask. I've saved the whole thing. You can see in a couple of minutes what I've been talking about. Won't you do that for me?"

Chad looked at his brother and smiled a bit. He had seen this stubborn streak before. He knew Ryan wouldn't stop until he got his way, though Chad hated giving in yet again .

"All right, already," Chad conceded wearily. "Let's look at it. Okay? Are you happy now?"

Ryan started to head toward his room.

The phone rang.

Chad waved Ryan on and answered it himself.

"Hello," he said.

"Is this the Bartlett residence?"

The voice was deep, intense, with a strange accent.

"Yes, sir, this is Chad Bartlett. Who's calling?"

Click.

"Hello, hello," Chad said before hanging up.

He stood there a moment.

Why would someone call and then disconnect a couple of seconds later?

"Who was that?" Ryan called out from his room.

"Wrong num . . . ," he started but stopped, remembering the caller's question:

Is this the Bartlett residence?

It couldn't have been just any stupid wrong number. The guy at the other end knew their name. He—

"Wrong what?" Ryan asked.

Chad didn't answer him right away.

"Hey, are you coming?" Ryan shouted.

"Yeah, right now," Chad replied.

"Then c'mon."

Chad knew he couldn't admit something just then to his brother.

His palms.

Suddenly they were sweating.

 # Four

Andrew Bartlett was covered with perspiration.

He never seemed able to get used to the Middle Eastern heat. Each day he spent in the region gave him more respect than ever for military personnel who had been assigned to duty in the desert.

The Muslims chalk it up to suffering for Allah, he thought. *The more they suffer, the more acceptable they think they are to Allah.*

He shivered at that idea. The difference between Muslim beliefs and Christianity were never more obvious to him: *They sacrifice themselves for Allah, and yet Christ sacrificed Himself for us.*

He looked about the dreary room. Dust and sand. There seemed to be a layer of it on everything—the chairs, the table next to him, the floor, even the windows.

And yet so many of the Muslims do seem happy.

Perhaps we could learn something at least from that.

He glanced at his watch. It was time. He opened his laptop computer and turned it on.

He had been given new information from a contact in a food market in the center of the city. It was contained on a disk which he slipped into the computer's side slot.

After a few seconds, the message showed up on screen:

TERRORIST PLOT CONFIRMED. HEAD BACK TO THE UNITED STATES. DO NOT DELAY.

Confirmed! But where? Andrew Bartlett asked himself.

The message continued:

IT WILL NOT BE AN ATTACK AGAINST WASHINGTON, D.C., AS ORIGINALLY REPORTED. SOME MINOR EXPLOSIONS WILL BE SET UP THERE AS FALSE ALARMS. THE REAL TARGET WILL BE—

He scrolled down to the next few lines:

—A NUCLEAR POWER PLANT IN SOUTHERN CALIFORNIA.

"Ryan and Chad!" he said their names out loud.

He almost instinctively reached for the old phone on the table but stopped and read the rest of the message:

SITUATION EXTREMELY DANGEROUS. TERRORISTS WILL ATTEMPT TO CAUSE A NUCLEAR DISASTER KILLING TENS OF THOUSANDS OF PEOPLE. THEY MUST BE STOPPED!

There was one more line:

BE PREPARED TO USE ANY AND ALL NECESSARY MEASURES.

He suspected he knew why he was being called back instead of the agency depending totally on the FBI and local law enforcement.

He was the expert.

He chuckled without any humor as he realized that that was what his superiors at headquarters considered him—the agency's top expert on the Middle East.

That's where these terrorists fall short, he thought. *They want to do it all themselves. They want all the glory. So it's not likely that they will hire people who are Americans, even though such assassins would have far less chance of being noticed.*

Usually Andrew Bartlett looked at the broad picture, at huge numbers of innocent people who were falling victim to the bloody tactics of terrorists and the governments who supported these madmen. He looked at war and sudden death. And he hadn't lost sight of any of that. But this time it was indeed more personal. With Southern California a target area, his sons could be involved, if only by being innocently in the line of fire.

He must do something to warn them, to tell them that even their home might not be safe this time. He had to try to get through by phone and leave some sort of innocent-sounding message, praying that his sons would understand his intent.

Since the day you were born I've tried to keep you safe.

Andrew Bartlett was thinking of the security measures that had been in effect during the many long years he had worked for the Secret Service. This was true not only when he was travelling in his cover job as a Special Envoy but also when he was back at home.

Even there, away from military secrets and spy cameras and hidden, ultra-sensitive microphones, "protection" was necessary, but it could not be total. It could not be absolute as they found out that one terrible morning three years ago.

For a few years at least, the Bartlett home had been a safe place. He could enter it and keep the outside world at arm's length. Then came that awful tragedy. . . .

The awful tragedy that took his beloved wife had changed everything. For that was the day when the terrors of his job invaded their home, and altered the family permanently.

If anything happens to Ryan and Chad, I—I don't know how I would handle it. Lord, Lord, I love them so much!

The phone service in Syria used creaky, ancient equipment. Even in the best of times, it was unreliable. Now when he desperately needed it to be functioning properly, it seemed to cease altogether.

Five minutes passed.

Then ten.

Fifteen minutes.

Twenty.

Half an hour.

He could not act too angry at the operator because undoubtedly the man would scream nasty words back at him. Then the operator would cancel the call, and Mr. Bartlett would have no hope whatsoever of reaching Ryan and Chad.

Forty minutes.

Forty-five.

I can't stay here! I've got to go. I—.

More than an hour later, he was still unsuccessful in completing the call.

Finally he knew he could not wait any longer.

As always, a schedule drawn up by someone thousands of miles away dominated his life. This time it was forcing him to head out to an isolated air terminal. He would have to leave it up to the plane's pilot to establish short wave radio contact with Paris or London as soon as possible, and then have someone from one of those cities make contact with the boys.

"Protect them, Lord, please," Andrew Bartlett whispered as he turned his head toward the peeling plaster of the ceiling, his words aimed far beyond that dreary little room. "Please keep my sons safe."

It would be many more hours before he would know how God answered his prayer.

 **Five**

Chad had been geared toward being physical for as long as he could remember. He walked at an early age and used his arms and hands to grip and lift objects much more quickly than most children. Ryan was just the opposite. He was so clumsy early on that his parents wondered if he had a muscular problem.

I always hated computers, Ryan always loved them, Chad thought as he lay in bed that Thursday night, looking up at the ceiling. *He couldn't hit a ball out of the backyard, but I could send it flying blocks away.*

He was falling asleep, trying to get what Ryan had told him out of his mind, trying to forget how nervous he also felt.

He slipped into a dream, a dream that was a kind of montage of some encounters he and his brother had had over the years.

One of these involved a plane hit by lightning. The boys were on their way to meet their father

36

for a vacation in Florida. Their plane crash-landed in the Atlantic Ocean just off the Florida coast. Help came within an hour, but two passengers were attacked by sharks during the rescue. In the midst of that nightmare, someone could be heard repeating the Twenty-third Psalm.

That dream cut to another encounter, this one in England, at Stonehenge.

"Evil," Ryan was saying.

"Yeah, I get the chills," Chad agreed.

"What really went on here?"

"Nobody knows. You've heard the theories like I have."

"Secret rites. Demonic stuff."

"For sure. What about the strange markings that have appeared in the field around Stonehenge? Those perfect shapes cut out of the ground?" Chad asked his brother.

"Well, a farmer has found several shapes cut out of his wheat fields," Ryan recalled as they sat down on a bench just outside the Stonehenge circle. "One morning, there they were—the night before, nothing! He called Scotland Yard for help, and detectives were sent within hours to investigate. They did some heavy-duty figuring, and came to the conclusion that it would have taken almost *a hundred people* to do the same thing overnight. But there were no signs of *anyone!*"

"Fascinating," Chad said impatiently. "Let's check it out!"

That was the trip during which they were separated and Chad was kidnapped by a group of devil worshipers. . . .

"I feel a mite guilty about this," Miss Stephenson said, her British accent as thick as ever.

She was taking some time off to be with her visiting parents for the weekend.

"Don't feel guilty," Chad had told her. "You've been working hard."

Both boys were at the breakfast table.

"But your father wants me to look after you," she replied. "Although—." She looked at them both and rubbed her chin.

"What were you going to say?" Ryan asked.

"Well, I must admit, you two seem far more respectable and honest and resourceful than any young people I've ever known!"

"That's because we're not so young," Ryan added.

"You aren't?" she asked, as gullible as ever.

"Actually we're nearly a hundred years old."

Her eyes widened.

"One of Dad's experiments, you know," Chad put in. "You just can't imagine what these diplomat-types are into anymore."

Her cheeks turned a rosy red as she blushed.

"All right, all right," she said, smiling at the same time. "Very funny, you two blokes."

"Seriously, have a good time," Ryan told her.

"I will, I will," she assured him. "I'm an old maid, yes, but I do have my parents who live in England. And I'm still a little shocked that Mumsy and Daddy just decided to take this sudden holiday here in America."

She kissed Ryan on the cheek, then Chad, and waved as she left.

I wonder if she, too, works for the agency, they both had thought at one point.

"Ryan?" Chad asked after Miss Stephenson was gone.

"Yes," Ryan said, looking up from the large bowl of milk-soaked cereal in front of him.

"Those printouts you showed me?"

"What about them?" he asked, trying not to be sarcastic. "You can't believe they mean anything, can you? What's the point of even talking about them?"

"It *is* bizarre, yes, but let's say, just for a second, that we've intercepted something really important."

Ryan could see that there was something going on inside his brother. And there could be no doubt that whatever it was had to do with that mysterious and alarming computer message.

"You look tired this morning," Ryan observed. "Didn't you sleep good last night?"

Chad blushed.

"What makes you think that?" he asked.

"You're blushing. That tells me a lot."

"Well, all right, I didn't. I was dreaming."

"So was I, for what it's worth," said Ryan. "Rough stuff . . . like remembering that plane crash in the Everglades."

"I'll bet you also dreamed about the Stonehenge stuff," Chad interrupted.

"Is that what you dreamed about?" Ryan asked.

"Yeah," said Chad, "but I didn't dream about what happened yesterday."

"You only *think* you didn't."

"How would *you* know?" Chad said, forgetting for a moment that his brother had a genius IQ.

He waved his hand through the air and added, "All right, all right, don't remind me. So go ahead and explain, will ya?"

"When we're nervous or scared or whatever," Ryan said, "we sometimes go back in our dreams to other times in our lives when we were also nervous or scared. Or we might make up some new stuff. The idea is that *something* is triggered in our subconscious mind, and that's how nightmares are born."

"I thought you were into computers, not psychiatry. "

"I'm full of surprises, Chad."

"I bet you are."

40

Ryan reached across the table and put his hand on his brother's arm.

"Why don't we just forget yesterday?" he said softly. "We don't have school today because of that teachers' meeting. So let's get some stuff done around the house. For what it's worth, I'll even help you with the never-ending list of things you're always doing to your bike."

"Oh, that'll be a lot of help!"

"Don't be sarcastic," he said forgivingly. "Anyway tonight we can load ourselves up with lots of pizza and catch a movie. How about that?"

"But you were so concerned about this so-called terrorist business," Chad replied.

"That was then, this is now. C'mon, what do you say about tonight?"

Chad smiled as he nodded, realizing he sometimes felt like the younger brother.

"Great," he said. "That's a plan. I like it."

After they'd come home that night, Ryan decided to work with his computer.

Maybe I can get something together that'll convince even Chad, he told himself. *Just maybe. . . .*

He turned it on and paused, trying to remember what he had been doing before he linked in with that earlier, disturbing signal.

Yes!

He had been trying to reach his father's computer, first at the office, and then he was going to switch to the remote in the laptop that was with Andrew Bartlett practically wherever he was.

If he could make contact and get his father to call him, he'd sure feel better.

On screen he typed the access code, a special one that nobody else outside the agency itself had.

During the few seconds he was waiting for the response, he recalled how excited his brother and he were when they learned what their father did for a living.

Spies and international secrets and all that stuff. Dark corridors in old buildings in strange countries. Knives and guns and lurking—.

The connection was made.

Wait a minute!

He picked up a telltale beep. That meant—.

It was a "secret" his father had told him about a year or so earlier. That one little beep, which could have been easily overlooked, told him what he needed to know.

"Thanks, Dad," he whispered, glad that listening for such a sound had become second nature for him.

What it revealed seemed more chilling to him than some ice cubes jammed down his back.

It meant that someone else had patched into the line at the same time!

Maybe Dad's trying to access it for any electronic messages.

He suddenly pushed himself back from the computer, his eyes widening.

Man, you're really losin' it. We can't both be on the line at the same time.

The implications made him shiver. But he had to be sure. That was something else Andrew Bartlett had taught his son—the need to be careful and absolutely certain.

He disconnected and waited about five minutes. His heart started beating faster, faster, faster.

It was the longest five minutes he had experienced in some time.

He typed the access code again, one number at a time, very slowly, and then the identifying letters: A . . . B . . . T . . . P . . . R . . . C

Then the computer at the other end responded: ANDREW BARTLETT.

TOP PRIORITY RESTRICTED CLASSIFIC–A–T–I–O–N.

Beep!

He shut down the computer instantly. His hands were shaking.

"Tapped!" he said out loud. "It *is* being tapped. It really is!"

The line had been intercepted somehow and—.

"Ryan . . ." his brother's voice was nearby. Ryan spun around on the swivel computer chair. Chad was standing in the doorway.

"I heard you in here and wanted to see what was cookin'," he said. "Been here for maybe five minutes or so, just standing. You were so involved you never noticed."

Chad walked over to his brother.

"Ryan, I saw what was going on. A private agency line has been violated."

Ryan nodded, swallowing with great difficulty.

"We can't reach Dad," he remarked. "I couldn't get through at all. But we can't just sit here and do nothing."

"There's Dad's confidential code—the one only for emergencies," Chad reminded Ryan.

"You're right, he did say we could use it in an emergency. But it's at the bank in the safe-deposit box. We can't get to it until morning."

Ryan's mind was whirling with what might be going on. He closed his eyes for a moment, rubbing the lids. Then he opened them and looked straight up at his brother.

"Chad, is this for real?" he asked. "Are . . . are we . . . I mean, are we missing something here?"

"We can't take a chance," Chad replied. He smiled slightly as he realized that their positions had reversed. Now Ryan was trying to play the part of the skeptic.

"You're right," Ryan agreed after a second or two.

He shut off the computer and stood.

"What a mess," he mumbled. "What a mess!"

Ishtar was pacing nervously.

"Did they lock in on it?" he asked.

"Wait," Mohammed said irritably. "I'm waiting to find out."

The message he had been hoping to get now appeared on the computer screen.

"Look, Ishtar!" he said excitedly.

The other rushed over and read those same words:

MYSTERY SOLVED. SOURCE LOCATED. WE CALLED THEM ONCE TO VERIFY, THEN HUNG UP. SHOULD BE TAKEN CARE OF BEFORE THE PASSAGE OF ANOTHER DAY. SEE TO IT, BOTH OF YOU.

They looked at one another and threw up their hands in a gesture of celebration. The transmission ended with the name and address they needed.

 **Six**

At first, Chad intended to take the motorcycle.

"No!" Ryan told him. "I like the look of it and all that, but it's scary. I mean, we could be killed on it."

"Think of how many people are killed in cars each year," Chad reminded him, replaying a stale old argument.

"I think we should go in the car, Chad, I really do."

His brother gave in, and they took the car.

Someday, Chad thought, *someday, you're not going to get your way, Ryan.*

Both Bartlett brothers were glad the bank they used was open on Saturday. On their way there, Ryan kept looking in the rearview mirror. He was beginning to suspect they were being followed, but he didn't say anything. He didn't want to make Chad nervous. Besides, he couldn't be sure.

The two of them finally arrived at the bank.

It's still following us, Ryan thought nervously. *It's still—.* He glanced quickly at the other car as he and Chad were entering the bank.

They stopped outside! he exclaimed to himself. *They really are after us.*

"Chad," he said so low that his brother could hardly hear him.

"Yeah, what?"

"Don't look," he added nervously.

"Don't look at what?" Chad asked. "What is it now?"

"We're being followed."

"Are you crazy, or what?"

Ryan's expression was so intent that Chad knew the answer right away.

"Okay, okay. What makes you say that?"

"How many miles from our house to here?"

"Five, I guess."

"How many turns?"

"I don't know. A lot. There's no straight route."

"He's been right smack behind us on each one, Chad!"

Chad shrugged.

"Coincidence, Ryan. That's all."

Ryan looked cautiously over his shoulder. The car was gone.

"It's not there now," he admitted.

"Of course," Chad said, satisfied with himself.

Ryan shivered then as the two of them entered the bank and approached someone to help them. It took only a matter of minutes to get to the safe-deposit box.

After the bored-seeming teller had left, they just stood and looked at the dark gray surface of the box. Ever since their father had told them about it, they often had wondered what else might be inside it in addition to what they had just come for.

Running his fingers curiously over the box, Ryan said, "We've *heard* about this for so long I was wondering if we'd ever actually *see* it."

"Yeah," Chad said absent-mindedly, equally as anxious as his brother to see what was inside.

"What'll we do if—?" Ryan started, but Chad interrupted him.

"It'll be there. Dad said so. That's good enough for me. How about you?"

Ryan was blushing.

"You're right," he said. "Let's get on with it."

"Exactly!"

Most of the adventures they had experienced had been away from home. This current mess was only the second threat they had ever felt right in their own backyard. The first had been their mother's death when her car exploded.

Ryan felt the need to explain himself.

"I guess I'm more upset than I thought," he offered.

"You got that right," Chad replied with real impatience. "Now open the box, okay?"

Ryan did just that. Attached to a wide metal clip in the lid was the phone number they needed.

"Let's go," Ryan urged. Although he was curious about the rest of the contents, he was more anxious to use the number and contact his dad.

"Wait," Chad said. "Let's see what else is here."

"I'm just as fascinated as you," Ryan told him. "But we've got to *move!*"

"Just a couple of minutes," Chad added. "How can that hurt?"

Clippings. News stories of governments overthrown. And political assassinations.

"Assassinations, Chad," Ryan said. "What in the world makes Dad save that stuff?"

"You're thinking he might have been involved?"

"Well, yes. It's not unknown in the work he does, after all. Why else would he have this collection?"

"Hey, let's not accuse him until he's here to explain, okay?"

Ryan nodded sheepishly, embarrassed.

In addition to the clippings, there was a sealed envelope. Typed on the front were the words: IN THE EVENT OF MY DEATH.

Chad seemed ready to open it.

"Don't!" Ryan protested.

"Aren't you curious, too?" Chad asked.

"Yeah, of course. But Dad trusts us. He doesn't want it opened now. There's got to be a reason. Let's respect his wishes."

His brother nodded.

There seemed to be nothing else of interest in the safe-deposit box, and Chad was about to close and lock it.

"Look," Ryan said, pointing to a small, square, transparent box in one corner.

Chad reached in and lifted it out.

Pills.

"What in the world?" he said, scratching his forehead. "Dad's not some speed freak. So what are—?"

"Cyanide," Ryan said.

"Are you kidding?"

"No."

Chad saw that his brother *was* serious.

"Spies have to have these within reach at all times," Ryan said, recalling what he had learned some time before.

"How do you know for sure, Ryan?"

"Info from that diplomatic news service."

Chad was shaken and almost dropped the plastic container. Ryan took it from him and put it back inside the safe-deposit box.

"Are you all right?" he asked.

Chad shook his head.

"I'm not, Ryan, I'm not all right. They're suicide pills."

"I know."

"How can you be so calm? How can you stand there and be so calm knowing that Dad might have to . . . to—?"

Chad couldn't say it.

"I'm not calm," Ryan admitted. "My stomach feels like it's about ready to—."

The words were choked off as he tried to steady his nerves.

Seconds passed before either of them could say anything else.

"I learned what I did from that news service," Ryan said, "but I just didn't connect it with Dad, at least not until now. I managed to blank it out somehow."

"Suicide is a sin, Ryan."

Ryan bowed his head, the sight of those pills burrowed deep into his mind. What could he say? His father would have to fill in the blanks later. There was no way they could judge him.

"Let's go," Chad said. "I've got to get some fresh air."

"Yeah," Ryan replied. "I need some, too."

They pushed a button on the wall near the heavy, reinforced entrance. The teller returned immediately.

As they turned to leave, the teller said, "By the way, I would be careful if I were you."

"About what?" Ryan asked nervously.

"There was a Middle Eastern looking guy . . . he did seem like he was trying to get into your car. But I scared him away."

The brothers exchanged glances.

"Sir, could we use one of the bank's telephones?" Ryan asked. "This might be urgent."

"Sure," the teller replied. "Follow me."

Using his dad's confidential code, Ryan got through to the agency almost immediately.

They were told to stay at the bank.

Both boys remained inside, waiting for an agent to come and get them.

Being the sons of Andrew Bartlett turned out to be a big help for them at the agency's central office. The number they called apparently was more special than they could have imagined. As soon as the individual at the other end realized who they were, they got immediate cooperation.

"Be calm," the nameless man said.

"We are calm," Ryan told him.

"That's good. I'll have someone over there in a few minutes."

"Thank you."

"No problem. Anything for Andy Bartlett's kids!"

Ryan hung up and told his brother what the man had said.

"Dad must really be something there," Chad remarked.

"He always talks about being proud of us. We're going to have to tell him how *we* feel about him."

"Agreed!"

Twenty minutes passed and the two were getting bored. There was nothing to do but sit around and watch the various customers come and go. Yet, with help on the way they were beginning to relax a bit. Little did they know that the danger was just beginning. . . .

Ishtar had driven the car around to a side street.

"This is crazy," Mohammed said, trying to convince Ishtar that the plan he offered was outrageous. The dangers outweighed any benefits.

"But that is not so. We have far too much at stake here. There is no other choice. We have no alternative, Mohammed."

"You are wrong. We should give it up altogether and wait for further instructions."

Ishtar hesitated. Mohammed spoke some truth. There had been no planning for what he suggested. As they sat in their car, they had little enough idea what they would find inside. Any such plan truly was insane. Yet they also didn't know why it all was taking so long in the large, white-marble building across the street. What if the two American teenagers were making contact with—?

"We can't risk a delay," Ishtar said finally. "Too much could be sacrificed if we do."

Mohammed resigned himself to following orders, even if these seemed suicidal.

The two scruffy-looking men walked into the bank.

There were about fifteen customers waiting in line at the various teller stations. A uniformed guard stood to one side of the entrance.

The clock on the far wall read 10:53.

"Look!" Ryan said.

Chad glanced in the direction his brother had been nodding.

"Those two men seem nervous," Chad said. "Is that what you mean?"

"Yes," Ryan agreed.

"So what?"

"Look at their hands."

"Yeah, in their coat pockets."

Chad's eyes widened as he realized what his brother was trying to tell him.

"That's not necessarily—," he started to say.

They were sitting at the desk of Martin Brisbane, one of the vice-presidents of the bank. He knew their father well, and he had tried to make them feel relaxed while they were waiting.

Brisbane soon picked up on how they were acting.

"Hey, guys, what's wrong?" he asked.

"Over there," Ryan said, whispering. "Those two men."

Brisbane stole a glance in that direction.

"What's wrong? They seem pretty rough types, but—."

The answer came seconds later.

There was a struggle between the guard and the two men.

The gun went off and the guard spun backwards against some startled customers, sending several sprawling on the marble floor, including an elderly woman in a motorized wheelchair.

Ryan and Chad ducked.

"Out the back exit," Brisbane told them. "Hurry!"

"Are you—?" Ryan asked.

"Yes! Now go!"

Ryan and Chad got down on their stomachs and started crawling toward the exit Brisbane had indicated.

To cover their real intentions, the intruders approached teller after teller, loudly demanding money. The frightened tellers didn't resist. They quickly handed over whatever they had in their locked cash drawers.

Unnoticed, Brisbane had gotten a Smith and Wesson revolver out of the bottom left drawer of his desk.

Two clear shots—that's all I need, he thought.

He got one.

That shot caught the larger of the two men in the neck. He fell instantly, a gurgling sound escaping his lips.

The other man spun around and started firing haphazardly. Several men and women were wounded.

"I've got to get those kids!" he babbled. "They can't get away. They—."

The intruder caught a glimpse of Ryan and Chad standing briefly as they reached the exit, and he started running toward them.

Martin Brisbane had dropped to his knees, holding his revolver straight out in front of him.

It took three shots before the onrushing man fell, a look of surprise and pain on his face. He landed on top of Brisbane's desk.

Brisbane stood and hurried up to him, trying to find some indication of a pulse.

There was none.

"See to the wounded!" he shouted. "Get some ambulances over here. Now!"

He turned to Ryan and Chad.

"Are you okay?" he asked.

"Fine," they both said at the same time. "Not a scratch."

As it turned out, no one had fatal wounds except the two men who had started all the shooting. Even the guard would soon recover.

 **Seven**

Why is it taking that agent so long?" Chad asked impatiently as he looked at the scene spread out before him, the confusion only then starting to die down.

"I'm beginning to wonder myself," Martin Brisbane said.

"Should I call—?"

"No," Brisbane interrupted. "He'll be here. Have patience, my friend."

They were now in the bank president's office.

"How come you had a gun handy, sir?" Ryan asked, realizing how curious that was.

"Ask your father someday," he said simply.

"Talk to Dad about it?" Chad remarked. "What does he—?"

His eyes widened. So did Ryan's.

"Are you—?" Chad started to ask.

Brisbane nodded.

Chad sat back against his chair.

A bank manager . . . a diplomat . . . who knows how many others with everyday jobs, were actually—!

"Everywhere, son," Brisbane added. "You'd be amazed how many and where, trust me."

"But why?" Chad asked. "I don't understand."

"Because the threat itself is everywhere. These days it comes not just from one particular source."

The rest of the answer had come not from Martin Brisbane but, surprisingly, from Ryan.

Chad turned to his brother, listening.

"Terrorists have been entering the United States at a faster pace than ever before. They come in mostly from the Middle East, but there are also some from the Orient and other locations. They seem to lay low for a period of time, then strike without warning."

Chad was more impressed than he could ever allow himself to admit.

"You sound like Dad would, saying the same thing," he pointed out.

"Is that bad?"

"Of course not, Ryan."

"It's not only terrorists, as such," Brisbane added. "When the Cold War with the Soviet Union ended, that was supposed to bring worldwide peace, yet most countries still maintain their spy networks."

"Like Dad?" Ryan asked.

"Like all of us, my young friend, like all of us."

"You said that the terrorists lay low for a period of time," Chad said to his brother, "and then they strike. But I haven't heard of any incidents like that. I mean, bombs going off in this country, stuff like that."

"Are you so sure?" Brisbane answered in Ryan's place. "How many planes have crashed with no explanation in the last two years? How many train derailments have there been? How many warehouses have gone up in smoke? Add up the number of not-quite-completed apartment complexes that become piles of ash and blackened timber."

"Are you saying that there is an undeclared war of some sort going on?" Chad asked.

"You could call it that, and not be very far off base, yes."

Brisbane cleared his throat.

"And the drugs, too," he continued. "Terrorists are after control of the drug scene. Next to some of these guys, Al Capone would seem like Mother Teresa."

"Don't the mafia and the Colombians have that stuff all tied up?" Chad remarked.

"It's changing," Brisbane said. "Certain terrorist groups from other parts of the world are moving in. They know if enough Americans get hooked on drugs, the country will collapse from the inside out."

"Have we stumbled into something really big here, sir?" Ryan asked uncertainly, thinking of what he had just uncovered through his computer at home.

"That's hard to say. It may be nothing at all. But sure, that's a possibility. It might well be the start of new terrorist activities in the United States."

"You talk as though you have no doubt that all this *will* get worse," Chad pointed out. "Are you so sure, sir?"

"Indeed we are," Brisbane answered. "But even if I'm wrong, and I certainly could be, the *present* level of activity is intolerable. People are dying all across this nation. Yet, because of the likelihood of public panic, we cannot make any outright announcements as to what really is going on. Instead, I'm afraid that we have been forced to go ahead and label the incidents as mishaps, accidents, nothing more than that."

He leaned over to the two of them, lowering his voice even though there was no one else in the office with them.

"But I am convinced that there *is* more to what we are seeing day after day. A plane crash. A train flying off its tracks. An oil refinery fire. A warehouse burns to the ground. These and other incidents are just part of a larger picture, my friends. And *that is* what continues to cause me sleepless nights."

One car explodes . . . and their mom is killed.

Yes they knew exactly what Martin Brisbane was talking about.

The agent's name was Bryan Winters. In his mid forties, he looked much younger, red hair cut to prescribed length, some freckles on his cheeks. He had finally arrived at the bank, and after thanking Martin Brisbane, he went outside with Ryan and Chad.

"Point out your car, guys," he asked.

They showed him where it was parked.

"I'll follow you home, okay?"

"That'll be fine," Chad said, knowing they had little choice in the matter.

An hour later Agent Winters was looking at the computer printouts as he sat in their living room. Both Ryan and Chad noticed that he had an impatient manner about him.

"Interesting," he said, yet his tone of voice seemed more bored than anything else.

"Interesting?" Ryan repeated the word. "That's all?"

"It's probably a fluke," Winters told the two of them. "This sort of thing isn't unusual, you know."

"Aren't you going to check it out?" Chad asked.

"Sure we will," the agent said as he got to his feet. "Let me assure you that we *do* appreciate your help."

Chad and Ryan glanced at one another and then back at Winters.

He shook hands with them and then left.

"Winters didn't seem very excited," Ryan observed.

"To him, we're just two kids," Chad said.

They were upset for the rest of the morning.

"It's a good thing we didn't have school today. What would we have told the principal?" Chad asked. "That a terrorist activity we thought we could expose probably will turn out to be nothing. Think he'd believe that?"

Ryan laughed at his brother's manner.

"I'm funny now, is that it?" Chad said.

"Sorry, sorry," Ryan told him. "You look like I feel."

"If ever we needed Dad!" Chad said, throwing his hands up in disgust.

That was one of the problems in living like they were forced to do. Too often they had to think and behave entirely like adults when they were in fact "just" teenagers.

"If only Dad would remarry," Ryan remarked.

He immediately regretted saying that. Chad took one look at him and then almost ran to his room, slamming the door angrily behind him. The entire house shook when the door closed.

It was not the best of all worlds for the two of them, though other teenagers would have given their eye-teeth to be on their own as much as Ryan and Chad. Of course, Miss Stephenson was usually around, but they could do just about anything they wanted, just about anytime they wanted. It went with the territory, forced on them by the job their father was doing.

If only Dad would remarry . . .

That definitely was the wrong thing to say just then, but it was hardly something they hadn't at least thought about. No one could take the place of their mother. And yet, the house felt empty more often than they liked to admit, an emptiness that still hung over it even when their father was with them.

If only . . .

Ryan shrugged his shoulders. They couldn't run their lives by the "if onlys" that kept popping up. They had to deal with what was, and doing so sometimes required a maximum amount of faith. Faith was often all they had to guide them.

Ryan headed toward his brother's room, knocking on the door when he got there.

"C'mon in," Chad called out to him.

Once inside, Ryan started to apologize.

"Don't sweat it," Chad told him. "This is tough on both of us."

He hesitated for a few seconds, then: "Ryan, maybe we should encourage Dad to start dating again. You know, maybe we've been a little at fault that he hasn't."

"What do you mean?" Ryan asked.

"It's kind of like body language, I guess. We never talk about it, so maybe he's thinking we don't want him to. Maybe we've given him the impression that since no one could ever take Mom's place, there was no point in anyone *trying* to do that."

Chad was looking at the framed snapshot of his mother on the nightstand beside his bed.

"Think of how lonely Dad must feel sometimes, even when he's home here."

"Yeah, the memories of Mom. And when he's away, it must be real bad."

They looked at one another.

"When he's back home this time, and it's gotta be soon, we'll talk, okay?" Chad asked.

Ryan nodded in agreement.

"For sure," he said, "for sure."

Bryan Winters could scarcely believe the way things had turned out. He had been alerted in his region to be on the lookout for something like this. And now it had fallen into his lap.

On the way to the office he stopped at a pay phone. He dialed a number so hastily that he made a mistake and got a pizza parlor instead. Then he redialed and finally made the right connection.

"This is Grizzly Bear," he said, using a code name.

"Have you turned up anything?" the voice at the other end asked without emotion.

"I have," he said. "I know exactly where they are. I can verify what headquarters told you."

"Good. We will meet right away."

"I can't come now. I have to be at the office today. But you don't need the printouts. Just believe me when I say they've got everything. You *must* take care of them before they become impatient and go to someone else or take it to the media."

"Yes, yes, the media. That would be very bad, as you say."

"Here's the address."

If we can get them at school or—."

"No," Winters interrupted. "Too public. Enough of that routine. Too much chance that something could go wrong at school. It's got to be right out of their own house, sudden, unexpected. If you do it right, it'll be awhile before anyone begins to realize these kids are missing. But it must be soon."

"All right, all right."

"And, Hoshyar, look over their place thoroughly. It's a very ordinary house. No hidden passageways. Make sure there is nothing left behind that would blow the lid on what we're planning."

"It will be done as you say."

"I mean it. There's another reason."

"What is that?"

"Their father."

"What about their father?"

"He works for the agency," Winters told him.

The other man whistled nervously.

"And there's something else, Hoshyar."

"He's just been given clearance to head back to the United States. He will be here in a couple of days."

"What caused this?" the one named Hoshyar asked.

"There are rumblings but no direct evidence."

"Rumblings? I don't understand."

"That's an American expression for hints, clues, suspicions. Get the message now?"

"Yes, yes. And he's returning on the basis of that?"

"As far as I can tell, yes. But then he's been away a long time. He has two sons waiting for him. Andrew Bartlett needs little more encouragement than that."

"We will hurry," Hoshyar assured him. "Allah will give us the victory."

The connection was broken.

Winters left the telephone booth and walked around his car to get in on the driver's side.

A man in a long coat had been standing across the street, trying not to draw attention to himself. As

Winters' car pulled away from the curb, he got into his own and followed.

Winters looked into his rearview mirror.

They know something's going on, he told himself. *Hoshyar and his buddies had better do it right.*

Suddenly he felt a chill at the base of his spine.

I may not be around much longer to help them.

He reached into his coat pocket, took out a little plastic container, glanced at the single pill inside.

It's supposed to be fast. . . .

That thought did nothing to make the chill go away.

 **Eight**

Why did you think he acted so bored?" Ryan was asking as they sat in the school gymnasium. It was Saturday afternoon, and Ryan had gone with his brother to a wrestling tournament.

"I guess one crazy idea ends up looking like another," Chad answered without taking his eyes off the wrestlers on the mat in front of him.

"But I thought you agreed—."

"I do, Ryan, I do, but then you can't blame Winters for reacting the way *I* first did."

"True," Ryan admitted.

Still, Ryan thought, *there's something about that guy, something that seems—.*

"My match is next," Chad said, getting to his feet and making his way over to the mat.

Ryan had to admit to himself that he envied a great deal about his brother. After all, Chad was five-feet-ten-inches tall, big-boned, and had the muscular build of a gymnast. He also happened to be extremely good-looking, with his wavy blond hair and well-defined body giving him the classic look of a surfer.

What am I in comparison? Ryan wondered to himself. *I'm three inches shorter than he is. No muscles. My bones show. He's the athlete, and I'm the geek with glasses, computer, and all.*

He sighed, realizing that these feelings were probably typical of such a situation. How many other guys felt like he did in other schools across the country? He guessed the number was not a small one by any means.

But my mind! Ryan thought. *Ah, there I run circles around Chad. There's no comparison between our IQ's. . . .*

Even then, he felt a little ashamed of himself. An air of pretense, of ego, that sort of thing, was just as wrong as any jealousy. Besides, Chad was no dummy. He made fairly good grades. He just wasn't interested in school work.

Actually they had talked about "the situation" from time to time. And Ryan had once picked up on a signal that Chad himself was envious of Ryan's intelligence.

How ironic! he thought as he watched his brother struggling on the wrestling mat that Saturday afternoon. *Each of us envies the other for exactly the opposite reasons!*

But there was something else he realized, then, seeing Chad being nearly pinned on the mat by his opponent.

I love the guy. I don't want anything to happen to him. I feel like rushing over to the bruiser on top on him now and shouting, "Stop it, you big slob. That's my brother. Don't hurt him, hear me? You'll regret it if you do!"

Ryan chuckled, mentally comparing himself to the wrestler who was giving Chad such a hard time, the images of a fly on the hide of an elephant coming to mind.

Eventually, the match was over and Chad ended up winning.

Ryan was elated.

Chad had a date after the tournament. A cute, bubbly cheerleader was waiting for him outside the locker room. Ryan caught up with a group of his friends and went out to eat.

After church on Sunday, both boys went on a picnic with the youth group. By Monday things really seemed back to normal. That is, until just before school ended for the day. Homeroom was the last half hour. So Ryan tried to concentrate on a computer magazine he had brought with him. He was considering switching from IBM to a Macintosh. However, he was uncertain and wanted to study all he could about both systems. He accidently knocked his pen to the floor. As he got up to retrieve it, he stood for a moment looking out the classroom windows.

Not much activity that time of day. In half an hour, well, that would be another story altogether. Then he saw the large black car parked at the curb in front of the school building, and he noticed someone standing outside, leaning on the hood.

That's one tough-looking guy, Ryan thought. Then as he was about to turn away he saw the others. Three of them inside the car.

Silly, he told himself. *Overly suspicious again. Knock it off, Ryan! Right now!*

His homeroom teacher, a woman in her late fifties named Mrs. Hutchinson, noticed that Ryan was acting strangely.

"Aren't you feeling well, Ryan?" she called over to him from her desk.

Embarrassed, he turned toward her.

"Just thinking," he said.

"About what?" she asked.

"Would you come over here, Mrs. Hutchinson?"

"Be glad to," she told him.

By now the other students in the class were becoming very curious as to what was going on.

Mrs. Hutchinson joined Ryan at the window.

"That car," he pointed.

She looked out the window at the vehicle.

"Mean-looking character, isn't he?" she said.

"What about the rest of it?"

She squinted her eyes.

"There are three other men waiting in the car."

"Seem strange to you, Mrs. Hutchinson?"

"Should it, Ryan?"

"Don't know. Just thought—."

Several of the other students got up from their desks and went to the window.

Suddenly the man standing outside hurried around the front of the car and hopped in on the driver's side. In just a few seconds the car had pulled away from the curb and was gone.

"We scared 'em off," one girl said, waving her hands in the air. "America saved for another day."

Ryan lost his temper.

"You act as though nothing bad could ever happen," he said. "This is just another game to you. But I gotta admit I sure feel better knowing that you actually have time to play the game between putting on makeup and deciding what outfit you're going to wear for the day! What an inspiration for the rest of us!"

He turned to the others.

"Everybody applaud her," he said, his voice raised. "She deserves it, doesn't she?"

Nobody said anything.

Lord, he thought. *This was wrong. I shouldn't have done it. I should be ashamed of myself.*

Realizing that he had been too extreme in his reaction, Ryan turned to the girl to apologize, and that was when he saw the tears in her eyes.

Chad could tell that there was something wrong with his brother. Ryan usually liked to talk a lot on the way home. But this time he was totally silent.

Midway there, Chad pulled the car over to the curb.

"All right, Ryan, what's going down?" he asked, concerned.

Ryan hesitated briefly, then told him.

Afterwards, Chad nodded, then said, "I guess that would bother me, too. I give some people the impression of being a little stuck-up, but I don't mean to. It's something I gotta work on."

He turned and faced his brother.

"But you don't have that problem, Ryan. Anyone in class who was aware of what happened will wonder what in the world was bugging you. They'll wonder why you acted like that, since it was nowhere near how you'd ordinarily handle things. I bet that girl will come up to you when she sees you the next time and be more worried as a friend than anything else. She'll forget her own feelings, just wait and see!"

Ryan looked at him with a surprised expression.

"Stop it," Chad said. "You act as though you're amazed that I could come up with anything like that."

"Well, I am . . . a little," Ryan admitted.

"Like if you would suddenly start lifting weights and doing fifty push-ups, is that it?"

"Yeah, that's right, I guess."

Chad started laughing.

"What is it?" Ryan asked.

"Oh, it just hit me how much alike we really are!"

Ryan smiled, enjoying the moment with his brother, then he turned abruptly serious.

"The car, those guys," he said, a frown forming. "I wonder if it means anything, Chad."

"I don't know for sure, of course; after all, I wasn't there with you, but I suspect it doesn't."

"But they looked so sinister!"

"Why do you say that, Ryan?"

"Because they did."

"But why?"

Ryan paused, thinking, then: "They were—."

He saw what his brother was getting at.

"—so foreign-looking! I—I can't believe I fell into that trap."

"You can't judge people that way. That's what Dad would say about now, isn't it? Besides, Ryan, remember this: The guys involved in this plot, they're on a secret mission, if those messages are to be believed. They probably wouldn't come out in the open like that. You think they'd kidnap us right from school? That wouldn't be very smart, would it?"

Ryan felt a chill.

"What if they're smart enough to expect all of this?" he asked, his voice unsteady. "What if they felt the obvious approach was actually the best, and that we wouldn't worry about it for that reason: because it was so obvious that we would have to end up guessing they wouldn't be so dumb?"

Chad looked at his brother with amazement. He had to admit that it would be real genius if the terrorists were to play on Americans' prejudices toward foreigners.

For Ryan, the chill he had felt a moment earlier continued without letting up at all. He couldn't get out of his mind the way those men looked, the mean expressions they had on their faces, as though they were waiting . . . *waiting to pounce once they saw their prey.*

 **Nine**

Ryan stood on the front porch, looking at the motorcycle parked in the driveway. Chad had brought it out of the garage after parking the car inside. A ray of moonlight bounced off the shiny metal that Chad had worked so hard to polish last weekend.

It brings out the cowboy in him, Lord, Ryan whispered to himself. *He gets on that thing, and he just gets reckless with it, driving up and down mountain curves at high speed, trying other crazy stunts.*

Ryan sighed with regret.

I sure don't want anything to happen to him. I—I—.

Ryan turned, then, and went back into the house. Miss Stephenson was in the kitchen.

"Want a snack?" she asked.

"Sure," he said. The thought of some cherry pie and cold milk sounded good.

Chad looked at the clock beside his bed—11:30 P.M.

He had just returned from jogging. He was still wearing his baggy sweats. His mind was ajumble with what his brother had managed to detect, and he had plopped down on his bed.

Ryan. . . .

Chad kidded him a lot, but he loved Ryan. Though he never seemed to admit it directly to his brother, he was proud of the little egghead.

He'll go on to do great things, Chad thought. *But me . . . I . . . I just don't know.*

He really believed that his brother would become a notable electronics engineer or develop some revolutionary new computer system that would change the whole industry. He suspected Ryan could end up calling the shots for whatever profession he wanted.

"We're talkin' big bucks for that kid," he whispered.

But Chad just wasn't sure of what would become of himself. Athletics would take him only so far, unless he got into pro sports or went the Olympics route, though he'd heard that guys who wanted to enter that competition usually started when they were much younger.

What else do I want to do with my life? If I'm not wrestling or playing basketball or—?

There was still no answer, not even much of a clue.

Ten years from now, when Ryan's famous, where will I be?

Oh well, he thought, *at least the Lord knows what's in store for my life.*

Chad took a shower and tried to relax. He was almost asleep when he started thinking again about Ryan's mysterious computer messages.

Muslim radicals will try a takeover....

Now those radicals had put two and two together and figured out that someone had "overheard" what they were planning.

They could be anywhere, Chad thought, *thousands of miles away or just across town.*

He could feel the muscles at the back of his neck tighten up.

They couldn't get to us that easily even if they knew who and where we were. If we see anything else suspicious, we could go straight to this Winters character and demand that he protect us.

Somehow thinking of that agent, dripping boredom as he did, didn't help Chad relax any faster.

Frustrated, he got up and went into the bathroom to get a glass of water. After drinking it down in one gulp, he headed back to his room when he paused, and listened.

It sounded like—!

A voice, low, cut off abruptly.

He shook his head, clearing it, and listened again.

Nothing.

Calm down, he told himself *It was the wind, maybe. Or something left over from crazy dreams. Or—.*

That final "or" sent chills tracing along his spine.

Ryan! That must be it! Talking in his sleep. These walls are pretty thin. That must have been what I heard.

A door's hinges creaking slightly. Then . . . nothing, only the normal quiet of night.

Chad smiled at how ridiculous he was acting.

A voice. Loud. Panicked.

Miss Stephenson!

Screaming in pain!

Ryan was still awake, dressed in a pullover sweater and a pair of jeans, when he knew that something was wrong.

Feeling restless, he went downstairs and stepped outside, pausing for a bit as he glanced at his brother's motorcycle. Then he had gone back in and headed for the kitchen, to get that glass of cold milk and some of Miss Stephenson's cherry pie. Finishing off the pie and taking his milk with him, Ryan had started back toward the stairs leading to the second floor when—.

Movement. The sounds of movement. And something else.

He glanced toward the large window in the living room.

A shadow, seen for an instant, then gone.

Whoever it was had been standing near the street light in front of their house.

He started to look away, but froze suddenly.

Another shadow, directly following the first. Then it also disappeared. Two shadows in themselves meant nothing: passing cars, tree branches stirred by a passing breeze, the list was not limited to just these possibilities. But the ones he saw were human in shape, and they seemed to be headed toward the side of the house.

His hand had begun to shake, and he saw that he had spilt some of the milk.

Slob, he chided himself, *and a nervous one at that. I'm beginning to see phantoms everywhere.*

Ryan had made it to the first step before he hesitated again.

A garbage can rattled for an instant.

Someone's in the backyard. I—.

He glanced up the stairs toward Chad's room, thinking that he should head straight there.

No. I'll go to the window in my room, look outside. . . .

Ryan gulped down what remained of the milk and put the empty glass carefully on a little square table to the left of the stairs. Next to it was also one of their telephones.

Should I call someone now? That agent? The man at the bank? Should I—?

He realized he had nothing very convincing to tell anyone as yet: Imagined shadowy shapes . . . noises that could have been caused by hungry neighborhood cats . . . that was about it.

He went slowly up the stairs to his room. Then he walked across to the window that faced the backyard and pulled the curtain a fraction of an inch to one side.

No one.

He waited a second or two.

Still empty. There was no one that he could see in the backyard.

Breathing a sigh of relief, he turned from the window. The wide-open window. . . . The window that he had closed minutes before, except for a one-inch slit at the bottom!

No one outside. No one there at all. And there was a reason for that, a very good reason. He sniffed. He could smell the odor of chewing tobacco, mixed with a trace of old sweat.

He turned his head just slightly. Out of the corner of his eye, Ryan could barely see two large shapes in the darkness, one of them just behind the opened door, the other in his closet, peering out.

He started coughing, a pretend cough, a cough that allowed him to disguise the fact that he had seen them both. He couldn't get past them. No way! He could only go straight ahead, which meant out the window, onto the roof of the back porch, and then down a flimsy vine-covered trellis to one side.

He started to lunge forward.

Suddenly a pair of hands grabbed at him. He kicked them loose.

Another arm came across his face and closed tightly.

If in doubt, bite, he thought, *right through to the bone if you have to go that far.*

He did.

Ryan could feel his teeth scrape against bone at the man's wrist. There was an audible cracking sound.

The man screamed in pain.

Now! Through the window. Act like your athletic brother for a change!

He was out on the roof and onto the trellis so quickly that even he was surprised.

Crack!

The trellis cracked and buckled under his weight. In the background, he could hear Miss Stephenson screaming.

Ryan landed on his back on soft grass. He jumped to his feet and started to run.

Someone had abruptly thrown open the front door and was rushing outside.

Ryan's eyes widened; then he sighed with relief.

Chad! Oh, Lord, thank you, it's Chad!

"Scram," Chad yelled. "My bike. Quick!"

Ryan objected, "What about Miss Stephenson?"

"We'll have to get help and come back. Now, hurry. Get on the bike."

Ryan bit his lip at the thought of riding the motorcycle he hated so much. But he jumped on just in time for it to . . . stall.

"Not *now!*" Chad protested. "Please, not now!"

The two men had run downstairs and were out the front door, heading right toward them.

"Shoot the kids!" one of them said. "You've got a silencer. Shoot them now!"

His partner took aim.

Ryan could feel something nick the corner of his left ear. The bike came to very loud life in that instant.

"We're outta here!" Chad yelled.

"Chad! Look!" Ryan warned him above the noise generated by the bike.

A third man was standing at the end of the driveway. He was large, with a gun that must have been chosen for its own bulk. He smiled as he took aim.

The gun jammed.

It happened in the movies but surely seldom in real life. Yet Ryan and Chad were glad that it happened at all, however illogical it might have been.

They were headed straight for the man who was now about to use the gun as a club, but Chad veered the bike to the right instead, and over the curb, into the street.

Other shots from other guns were now being fired at them, their telltale *popping* noises all that was heard through the silencers.

"We made it!" Ryan was shouting. "We actually made it!"

"Don't be so sure," Chad replied as he looked in his rearview mirror. "They're hopping into a car parked down the street. They're after us, Ryan. They *can't* let us get away now."

"It's no longer just some crazy kid's dumb imagination. We've got proof; right, Chad?"

"Right!"

Chad knew they couldn't get far before the men in the car caught them. He drove just two streets over to the home of a retired police officer named Barney Fitzsimmons. Chad guided the bike up the side yard and behind the garage so it couldn't be seen from the street.

Then they hurried up to Barney's back door, and knocked frantically.

Seconds passed. No response.

Then just as they were about to turn away, they heard footsteps inside.

"It's late, who's there at this time of night?" Barney's hoarse voice called out.

"Chad and Ryan Bartlett," Chad told him.

"What the dickens is wrong?" Barney said as he opened the door and glanced outside.

"We're being chased," Ryan said.

"Sure you are," Barney replied, unconvinced.

"By terrorists!" Ryan added, his eyes wide, frightened.

"By what?" the man burst out laughing. "It can't be drugs, not with you two. Tell me, what *is* wrong? I'm old. I'm retired. And I need my sleep."

"Do you still have your revolver?" Chad asked.

"Of course, I do," Barney admitted. "But what—?"

He looked at the two of them, studying them for a few seconds.

"This isn't a game, is it?" he said.

"No, sir. It's real, as real as—."

Screeching tires!

"How could they?" Ryan said, astonished.

"You came here on your bike?" Barney asked.

"Yeah, we did," Chad said.

"Tire marks then," Barney told them. There was a brief shower an hour or so ago. Everything's still wet. They must have been just behind you. Then followed your tire marks across the lawn. Inside! Pronto!"

He slammed the door behind them.

"Upstairs," he said. "Into my bedroom."

They followed him.

"You two, into the attic!" Barney motioned toward the trapdoor in the ceiling. "It has no windows, and only one entrance, in the master bedroom. They'll have to get through me first. There's an unused phone outlet in one corner of the attic."

He took a phone and flashlight from the night stand next to his bed.

"Take these. Call headquarters. Ask for—."

"Mulrooney?" Ryan said somewhat tentatively.

"Not that fat clown. Use my name. Ask for Detective Sam Jenkins. If he's not in, try Curtis, Detective John Curtis. Can you remember that, guys?"

They nodded in unison.

A crashing sound downstairs!

"Hurry!" Barney told them.

"Thanks, sir, thanks a whole lot," Ryan said. "Without your helping us—."

"I owe your father one," the ex-cop interrupted.

"Dad? You owe Dad—?" Chad started to say.

"That's it, for now. Get going!" Barney said urgently.

They grabbed the cord on the trapdoor leading to the attic and pulled down. As they did this, a set of ladderlike stairs extended toward them.

"Up! Now!" Barney whispered.

They were up the makeshift stairs in no time.

Both searched for the phone outlet. Ryan found it, plugged in the phone, and dialed police headquarters.

When someone at the other end answered, Ryan asked, "I need to speak with Detective Sam Curtis."

"Do you mean Sam Jenkins or John Curtis?" the voice asked, the tone hardly above a growl.

"Either one, *please!*"

"Don't get excited, kid. They're not here, anyway. Who's calling?"

"Ryan Bartlett."

"Yeah? What's wrong, Bartlett?"

The line went dead.

"N-o!" Ryan screamed.

"They cut the line didn't they?" Chad said.

"I guess that's it," Ryan admitted. "We've got problems then."

"That was a dumb thing to say. You think I don't know that by now?"

"But the guy at the other end. It was . . ."

"Not Mulroo—?" Chad started to say then stopped. The two of them looked at one another.

"That's right," Ryan said. "The one and only! Sergeant Mulrooney. He wouldn't believe in a terrorist attack if a bomb were planted under his—!"

"Lord, help us. . . ." Chad whispered.

"That's what it'll take," Ryan agreed. "We don't have anything else going for us right now."

A shot! Downstairs!

There were several more after that one . . . then a crash, like that caused by a large mirror knocked off a wall and shattering into a thousand pieces on the floor.

"We've got to do something, Chad," Ryan said. "What could we put on top of that trapdoor opening? We just can't let them barge on up here!"

They glanced about the attic.

At one end was an old chest of drawers. Hurriedly, they slid it over the trapdoor opening. Chad noticed something else.

A bow and arrows.

"A lot of good this will do us," he said, tossing it back on the floor.

Meanwhile the fighting downstairs continued.

A thud.

Barney's gravelly voice moaned loudly in agony.

Then utter, chilling silence.

 # Ten

"They've killed him," Ryan said. "Chad, they killed Barney!"

Ryan was no longer trying to be older than his years. He was then what he was: a scared fourteen-year-old.

And Chad was trying very hard to be one brave sixteen-year-old, to present the right image so that his brother could look up to him and see someone to be admired.

This had never really concerned him before. He was Chad Bartlett, period . . . to be taken for himself and not what was *expected* of him.

But now it was different. Both of them had to think like adults, for their lives would depend on exactly how they acted over the next few minutes.

"There's lots of stuff around here," Chad said. "Maybe we'll find something to help us."

Ryan came upon an old, rusty short-wave transmitter.

"If only it worked," he said. "But it probably doesn't."

Both stopped what they were doing. Footsteps downstairs. The creaking sound of springs.

"They've found the stairway," Ryan whispered. "They're on the way up!"

Chad glanced at the transmitter.

"Try the transmitter," he said anxiously.

"But it's useless," Ryan reminded him.

"*They* don't know that."

"Pretend time?"

"Yes, and we've got to do it better than ever."

They dragged the unit close to the trapdoor, and turned it on. It lit up, sure enough, but that was all.

"It's making a lot of noise," Ryan pointed out.

"Let's hope *they* hear it."

Ryan was used to transmitters, computers, and things like that, so he was the one to start using the unit.

"Mayday, Mayday!" he said. "Help me! Somebody help us."

The footsteps stopped.

"We are being attacked by several terrorists. I'll describe them and give the license number of their car. This is our address. Send help immediately."

Neither of them had seen the men, of course, but it was a good "pretend," and Ryan prayed that he was convincing.

Footsteps again. This time in the opposite direction! Then silence for several minutes.

"If too much time passes and nobody arrives, they'll smell a rat," Chad said.

"Maybe they've left already," Ryan suggested.

"Maybe . . . wait!"

Smoke. The distinct odor of wood burning.

No! Chad thought. *They haven't left. They're setting the house on fire.*

"We're trapped," Ryan said, his voice getting frantic. "We're actually trapped. They weren't fooled."

There were no windows in the attic.

"The air vent, Ryan, look!"

A triangle-shaped metal vent was inset at each side of the house right up flush against the top of the roof.

"Too small, Chad. *I* couldn't even get through there."

"But we can knock it out somehow, and then pry at the hole until it's a lot bigger."

Ryan looked at his brother.

"You're right. Why didn't I think of that?"

Ryan noticed a rusty old saw in one corner.

"Chad, look!"

"Perfect!"

But it wasn't. The old saw literally broke into pieces when they tried to use it.

The odor of smoke was more intense.

Ryan started coughing. He had had weak lungs for years, making him more susceptible than Chad would be. In a short while though, *both* of them could die from breathing the smoke, if not from the fire itself.

There was nothing else they could do.

They sank to their knees and prayed.

And no one knew where they were, except the men out to kill them. . . .

A helicopter!

"Chad! Listen!"

"I hear it, I hear it!"

A minute or two passed.

Sounds of a fight below them. Three shots fired. Then three more. Finally silence.

But only for a short while.

Footsteps.

"Oh, no!" Ryan said. "Are they coming back? Are they—?"

Chills traveled up and down his back. His brother and he glanced quickly at one another, their faces drained of color.

"Maybe we should get the bow and arrows," Ryan said, panicking. "Maybe—."

A voice. Someone was calling to them.

"Listen, Ryan! It sounds like—!"

"Yeah. Oh, God, please, let it be—."

It was. They quickly pushed aside the chest of drawers.

"Hello, guys," Andrew Bartlett said, smiling from ear-to-ear. "What a mess you've made this time."

After hugs and tears and an emotional prayer among the three of them, they finally went downstairs.

"Where's the fire?" Ryan asked.

"There was none, as such," his father said.

"But we *smelled* it, Dad," Chad protested.

"They found a large bucket and put some pieces of an old rug and some bunched up newspapers in it. Then they put the bucket under that trapdoor and set fire to the stuff."

"To smoke us out!" Ryan exclaimed.

"Burning down a house in a packed residential district would draw too much attention. They might not be able to get away in time. Besides, they certainly would be spotted and descriptions could have been provided by any number of eager witnesses. Foreign terrorists aren't exactly in favor these days!"

"Miss Stephenson!" Chad remembered. "Is she okay?"

"She is," Mr. Bartlett replied. "Tough lady, that one."

There was some movement in another room.

"I want to introduce you to someone," Mr. Bartlett told them. "It's as much because of him as your old dad that you two have come out of all this reasonably intact."

"Great," Chad said. "Who is it?"

"Bryan, would you come here, please?" Mr. Bartlett called out.

"Bryan? Uh oh," Chad whispered.

"Do you think—?" Ryan asked.

"Oh, do I!" Chad exclaimed.

"Guys, this is Special Agent Bryan Winters. I understand you already have met."

"Hello," Winters said as he stepped into the dining room where they were standing. "See, I'm not so bad, after all."

"We never, well, we didn't—," Ryan tried to say.

"Come on, you two, tell the truth. You thought I was completely out of it, didn't you? Man, were you wrong. I was more involved than you'd ever imagine!"

Within a matter of minutes, everyone in that immediate neighborhood and many others for blocks in every direction seemed to be converging on that house. By then the police had arrived.

Sergeant Mulrooney was one of them.

"Sir, can I tell you something?" Chad said to him.

"About how you thought I wasn't going to do anything?" Mulrooney said flat-out.

Chad's expression mirrored his amazement.

"Your brother sounded *real* upset," Mulrooney added, clearly enjoying the moment. "I *can* tell the difference between kids playing pranks or imagining things and someone in real distress."

Ryan approached the sergeant.

"Thank you, sir," he said. "You saved our lives."

"Actually I did very little. After all, we've only just arrived here."

"I don't understand."

"You see, as luck would have it—."

He saw Ryan frown.

"Okay, okay, as The Man Upstairs would have it, your father and somebody else stopped in only a few seconds after I talked with you. I told them about the call, and they left immediately. *Then* I called out my guys."

He smiled then.

"I would have done it anyway, Ryan," he said. "I like you both very much, I really do."

Their father walked over to them.

"Barney's going to make it," he said. "But—."

"But what, Dad?" Ryan asked.

"His back is hurt pretty bad. He'll probably have to have a considerable amount of physical therapy before he can walk again. Barney will need a lot of help from all of us. He'll be all right, but there's going to be some real pain in the process."

Mulrooney seemed nearly overcome with emotion.

"They did that . . . to Barney?" he said, as though repeating that was the most difficult task he had had to do in a very long time.

Mr. Bartlett nodded sadly.

"My wife and I, and then Jenkins and Curtis, yeah!" Mulrooney said thoughtfully. "We can shop for him. We can get him into a rehab situation as soon as he's regained his strength. We can help Barney, all of us sure can."

Ryan and Chad immediately volunteered to be added to the list. The sergeant told them that they would be first on his list, partly because they lived closer to Barney than anyone else did.

After Mulrooney had left, Ryan and Chad confessed to their father the image they had had of the man.

"That's called a preconception," he told them. "But then maybe you're not entirely at fault. Maybe Mulrooney once thought you were just crazy teenagers. What happened was that you ended up reinforcing one another's prejudices."

The two of them realized that their father had hit a bull's-eye again as far as human nature was concerned.

"The Lord has a habit of demolishing stuff like that," Mr. Bartlett told his two sons. "And then we stand back, amazed at ourselves and at Him, but for entirely opposite reasons!"

A voice interrupted, calling to them. It was Bryan Winters.

"We'd better be going," he reminded them.

The helicopter had been parked in the middle of the street, its motor turned off, its blades idle.

"Where *are* we going, Dad?" Ryan asked.

"A special treat," said Winters, jumping in before their father had a chance to answer. "We're going to our regional headquarters. It's not far from here. We need to get a complete report from you boys. You'll be going where few non-agents have ever gone before! How about that?"

Ryan was thrilled. Even Chad perked up at the thought.

"You just want to see their computer operation," he remarked.

"And *you* just can't wait to see what kind of gym equipment they have for the agents," Ryan said.

"Some things never change," their father said.

As they hopped onto the chopper, Ryan turned, and saw Sergeant Gavin Mulrooney waving to them.

"But some do," he said, "some really do."

Martin Brisbane was asleep when the phone call came through. He fumbled for the receiver, dropping it once, then managing to find it on the floor.

"Hello." he said, a terrible taste in a very dry mouth making it difficult for him to swallow properly.

"Bryan Winters is a double agent," the voice at the other end said abruptly.

Brisbane almost dropped the receiver a second time.

"How in the world do you know?" he asked.

He got a condensed version of the story: A group of terrorists had tried to kidnap or kill Ryan and Chad Bartlett. They were stopped just in time. One terrorist was fatally wounded on the spot. Another died on the way to the hospital. The third received only flesh wounds.

"Which one tipped you off?" Brisbane asked.

"The third guy," the voice replied.

"Was this Mulrooney's doing?"

"You bet it was. Nobody's better at this sort of thing."

"Best man we have in this whole region."

"Well, almost. . . ."

"After you, that is," Brisbane said, smoothing the other's ego.

"One big problem, though."

"You can't find Winters."

"No, the problem is we know *exactly* where he is."

"That's a problem?" Brisbane repeated, confused. "I must have lost track of something here."

"As we speak, Bryan Winters is in a helicopter with the entire Bartlett clan."

"What in the—?" Brisbane started to say, disgusted.

"I know. I know. I reacted the same way when I heard. Marty, we just can't rule out the fact that he suspects we now know the truth about him."

"And if he does, he might gamble on something desperate. Is that what you're saying?"

"Right on the money, Marty. Winters could very well go ahead and try a suicide mission directly at the nuclear power plant which his people intended to blow up in the first place!"

Suddenly it was even harder for Martin Brisbane to swallow.

If Winters cannot be stopped by persuasion, he thought, his head pounding wildly, *we'll—.* He hated the rest of the truth but knew it couldn't be avoided. *We'll have to stop him by blowing up the helicopter and everyone on it!*

At night the trip by helicopter was dazzling.

"It's been a long time," Bryan Winters remarked.

"What's that?" Mr. Bartlett asked.

"Oh, a long time since I was last in a bird like this one. Usually it's just the commercial airliners or somebody's ancient prop plane, slow and noisy to boot. But a helicopter, ah, that's a thrill."

"I guess it is," Mr. Bartlett agreed, "especially at night."

The chopper's radio came to life. Someone was trying to contact them.

Winters reached for the microphone.

"Hello, Unit 451 here," he said. "What's the problem?"

"You're off course. Turn back to the one that was authorized."

"Thanks for letting me know. Roger and out."

Winters glanced over at Andrew Bartlett next to him.

"Rustier than I thought," he said.

Ryan looked at the back of the man's neck. *Why don't I believe you?* he said to himself.

Less than a minute later, there was the same insistent voice on the radio.

"What's going on up there?" it said. "I *told* you—."

Winters shut the radio down in an angry motion that diverted his attention from steering the helicopter.

It lurched like a wounded beast, and started spiraling downward. Winters grabbed the wheel with both hands and steadied the flight.

"Listen, and listen good!" Winters said. "Nobody tells me *anything* these days, despite what that flunky said. Remember this, guys: I'm the only one here who can pilot this thing. I also have a gun and won't hesitate to fire it."

"What are you *doing?*" Mr. Bartlett asked after he managed to regain control of his stomach. "Bryan, you must know that this is utter madness!"

"Madness?" Winters repeated. "No, no! It's perfect sanity compared to what we will be destroying."

Ryan's mind went back to that first computer message interception.

"You're one of them, aren't you?" he blurted out. "You're part of this whole plan."

"Wrong!" Winters replied. "It's my plan to begin with, pal!"

"Plan?" Mr. Bartlett said, puzzled. "What plan are you talking about?"

"Tell him," Winters urged when Ryan hesitated. "Tell him what happened, *why* you all are involved."

Ryan recounted the details of the past few days.

Andrew Bartlett had heard some crazy stories over the years but few came close to equaling this one.

"But *why,* Bryan?" he asked. "You work for *us!*"

"Whatever *us* is, Andrew. It changes from administration to administration. I work for people who—."

"Who want a revolution in this country, isn't that it?"

"Of course. How *else* can we change things? And don't give me that ballot-box propaganda. Or any of your Christian mumbo-jumbo!"

"Just what do you think being a Christian—?"

"Can it," Winters said angrily, impatiently. "You see a fish to catch, and you've got your hook out for me already."

"I feel sorry for you, Bryan."

"Feel sorry not for me but for hundreds of thousands of doomed people when—." He bit off the rest of the words.

Hundreds of thousands of doomed people! Andrew Bartlett repeated those words in his mind, remembering the report that sent him back home in the first place.

The Los Arboles nuclear power plant! The report had it right. We're probably heading straight toward the plant now!

"You realize what this means, don't you?" he asked.

"Of course I do. It's a statement that needs to be made," Winters commented.

"On the backs of countless numbers of innocent people? Is that what you're saying, Bryan?"

"They're not so innocent, Andrew. They voted for those responsible for what is happening around the world in the name of democratic ideals. That makes them collaborators as far as I am concerned."

For several minutes they had been flying over an area with far fewer lights. Then suddenly they saw an intense concentration of light.

"Don't they know how much of a target all that makes the plant?" Winters remarked sarcastically.

"It's a trade-off, like having lights on the Empire State Building so that low-flying planes don't crash into it," Mr. Bartlett told him.

Winters started edging the helicopter downward.

"Don't, Bryan," Mr. Bartlett begged. "This is evil. You can't—."

Suddenly Chad lunged for the man's neck, his strong wrestler's arms accustomed to subduing an opponent. Bryan struggled to free himself from the teenager's grasp. Then Chad saw a shiny reflection flicker in the lights.

The gun. It went off.

A bullet hit Andrew Bartlett in the shoulder, the force of the impact at such close range flung him to the right, hard into the chopper door. The impact sprung open the clear, shatterproof door, and—!

Andrew managed to grab hold of a metal bar on the side. It was the one used for a rope to anchor the helicopter in extremely windy weather. His shoes and the lower part of his trousers had caught on a wide piece of rough bare metal at the bottom of the door frame. But they were tearing loose quickly as the middle part of his body was being pulled and sucked outward.

"Dad!" Ryan and Chad screamed at the same time.

 **Eleven**

The helicopter was clearly visible on the radar screen though Martin Brisbane had hoped that that would never be the case.

"We *have* to wait a minute or two longer," he pleaded. "We *can't* just blow them out of the sky. Andrew's too valuable—."

"I know how you feel." The joyless words came from Stefan Wilmott, the stern-looking man next to him, several steps up the agency's command ladder. "Don't you think I share your feeling? I'm not a robot, after all. But it's either Andrew Bartlett's death and his sons' or the deaths of a quarter of a million men, women and children, possibly a great deal more than that.

"In view of this, what choice do I have, Marty? Tell me that! Just give me *one* legitimate alternative, and I'll jump right in, and thank God for the opportunity!"

Brisbane nodded.

"Go ahead," he said out loud. "Do it now."

"I don't exactly *need* your permission, Marty!"

He turned to an assistant.

"Are they ready to take off?" he asked.

"Engines fired up and ready to go, sir."

"I want those planes in the air immediately. If that chopper doesn't change course dramatically in the next sixty seconds, you are ordered to make sure it ends up in a thousand little pieces, and that each one falls *outside* the boundaries of the plant."

"It's as good as done, sir."

Brisbane heard that. When his superior turned back to him, he remarked, "It may be necessary, yes. I might have to admit that, but don't ever call this matter good, don't you dare! We must never become so cold, so uncaring that we *ever* use such a word to describe what is going to be done here, not a day from now, not a decade."

The other man nodded sadly.

"You're right, Marty. Within the next minute or so, we stand to lose someone who's irreplaceable to the agency. And—."

He choked briefly with emotion, then cleared his throat and continued, "And a good and decent friend."

Both waited for the inevitable explosion that would be picked up by their radar screen. No doubt, it would be seen by witnesses on the ground for miles in every direction. People would remark about this latest air crash and then go on about their lives as before, never having a hint of the tragedy itself.

The shock of seeing what was happening to his father diverted Chad's attention from Bryan Winters who took advantage of this by instantly swerving the chopper to the left, back toward the power plant.

From nearby there came the rapidly intruding sounds of fighter jets!

Chad had only a split second to decide what to do.

The planes must have been sent to stop them from hitting the plant. They would have very little time to do so. With the nuclear generators only seconds away, the pilots would have to do something almost as soon as the chopper was in their line of sight.

His father was halfway out of the chopper. . . . Ryan, who had never lifted anything heavier than his computer, was trying to pull him back in but lacked the strength to do it.

"I—I can't hold on any longer, Chad—!" his little brother screamed in terror. "Dad managed to . . . grab something . . . on the side, but . . . I see blood. His fingers are—."

Chad wrapped both hands tightly together, forming a doublefist, and then hit Winters solidly across the back of the head. He hoped to knock Winters unconscious but stop short of breaking his neck.

The man groaned, then slumped, leaning left.

The chopper immediately started spinning out of control.

"Ryan, I'll get Dad," Chad shouted. "You fly this thing."

"*What?*" Ryan screamed back.

"Think of it as just another computer. Pretend you're playing *Flight Simulator.*"

As Chad was shifting over to the right side of the helicopter, he saw Winters out of the corner of his eye.

The guy's coming to! Oh, Lord, I didn't hit him hard enough. What do I do now? I need to know! What—?

"Chad, Dad's slipping more; he's—he's—," Ryan's voice penetrated his mind.

Lord, I can't do anything on my own. Help me!

He had been reaching out toward his father's legs, this position placing his own feet in Winters' direction.

Oh, God, Oh, God, be with me as I do this!

He kick-boxed the man twice in rapid succession, hoping to knock him out.

It happened a little differently this time.

The motion was so intense, so swift that Winters was flung against the opposite door of the chopper, which was ripped open as the one on the right side had been, and Winters tumbled outside, with nothing to stop him from plunging 12,000 feet.

Chad didn't have time to think about the expression of terror on the man's face. He frantically grabbed his father's leg, and Ryan scrambled past him and over to the pilot's seat.

"I don't know a thing about this, Chad!" he protested. "I—."

Except the radio transmitter-receiver!

His father had gotten him a top-notch shortwave unit for his twelfth birthday, and he had mastered it in record time!

Ryan reached for the radio microphone, dropping it in his haste and then searching for it in the near-darkness of the cockpit. Finally—.

"Mayday, Mayday," he repeated. "I'm Ryan Bartlett, and I'm fourteen years old . . . and I don't know how to be the pilot but I am, and . . . and I need help!"

Silence.

Lord, please, please, it's got to work. It—.

More seconds passed.

Ryan was beginning to feel that it was impossible, that he didn't know enough about how to—.

The radio crackled with static for a moment,

then: "This is Martin Brisbane, Ryan. I've flown helicopters before. Listen to me, son, listen to every word."

Praise God!

"Those planes, sir!" Ryan said desperately. "Can you stop the planes?"

"No problem, it's done. Now—."

Ryan knew that if he didn't follow instructions exactly, he might drift so close to the power plant that the jets would have to shoot the helicopter out of the air anyway.

Another possibility was that they could crash land on Pacific Coast Highway, a major traffic route!

Ryan realized there was only the slightest chance that he could ever land the unfamiliar aircraft without forcing its destruction one way or the other!

He seemed to be trembling all over as he listened to what Martin Brisbane was telling him. He prayed silently that he would be able to do what needed to be done if they were to survive.

As he struggled to control the helicopter, his mind drifted back to a scene from a few years ago. He and Chad and their mother were on a bumpy airplane ride en route from Washington, D.C., to Los Angeles. It was so bad, in fact, that passengers were screaming, several fainted, and one man had a heart attack from the stress.

"Of course, you're afraid," his mom had told them both. "There's nothing wrong with fear. But it must give way to absolute trust that, whatever happens, we have the assurance that God is going to be with us. Fear is easier than trust. It's a natural feeling. Trusting God takes more effort. But I know my kids. I know the two of you can do it!"

Ryan glanced for not more than a split second at his brother.

He's done it! He's actually—!

Chad's muscular arms had gotten ahold of Andrew Bartlett and pulled him back into the helicopter.

Thank You, Jesus, Ryan thought. *If the three of us die now, at least we'll do it together. . . .*

 **Twelve**

The next few minutes would always be a blur in their minds.

Ryan managed to bring the helicopter to a safe landing only after narrowly skirting some high-voltage wires a few hundred feet from the nuclear power plant.

Andrew Bartlett had to be rushed to a nearby hospital. The bullet wound was not serious in it-self, but he had lost a considerable amount of blood and needed to stay there for several days.

He was in a wheelchair, sitting on an open porch at the rear of the main hospital building, ready to go home.

I feel as old as I am, he told himself. *No, that's not it exactly. I feel older!*

He looked up as he heard the two familiar voices.

"Hello, guys," he said, greeting his sons.

How young they are, he thought. *They have fifty years ahead of them.*

"Dad?" Chad asked.

"What is it, son?"

"We've decided you're a great guy and all that, and we're going to keep you as our father," Chad remarked with as straight a face as he could manage.

"Now I *am* relieved to hear that from the two of you," Andrew Bartlett said, joining in on the joke. "In return, I guess I won't cancel the adoption papers after all."

They hugged one another, vividly remembering that as recently as four days ago, they could have been blasted out of the sky.

"Why did Winters do what he did?" Ryan asked as they were preparing to leave the hospital later that same morning.

"He was deceived," Mr. Bartlett said. "Martin Brisbane told me that they really don't have much more than that to go on, but he suspects it had something to do with the death of his wife."

"He lost someone, too?" Chad remarked.

"I'm afraid so," Mr. Bartlett replied. "After that, he went for the money. That terrorist organization was paying him a tremendous amount."

"Just the money, Dad?" Ryan asked.

"And a desire for revenge against the system that caused his tragedy."

"But you didn't turn out that way when Mom died," Ryan added.

"No, but then . . . Bryan Winters had no one else, no children, no—," he stammered.

"Dad, are you all right?" Chad asked.

"Oh, I am, son, I am."

"He didn't have Christ in his life, isn't that what you were going to say?" Chad commented.

"You're right, son, he didn't. He had no anchor. He was adrift. And he pulled into the wrong harbor. "

Those last moments with Winters in the helicopter flashed across Chad's mind. The look of terror on his face was something Chad would never forget.

"Dad, I killed him, didn't I?" Chad spoke with some effort.

"No, you didn't. You tried very hard to knock him out, but—."

"Without what I did, though, he might still be alive."

"You're forgetting one thing, son: If you hadn't acted that way, *none* of us would be alive right now. Or worse, he might have made it to the power plant, crash-landed into a nuclear generator, and caused a nightmare that would have hurt thousands of innocent people."

"I've been through all that in my mind, Dad, I really have. It'll take awhile to get over it all."

"That's happened to me," his father admitted, "not just once, but maybe a hundred times over the years."

Ryan and Chad obviously had something else on their minds.

"All right, all right, what is it, guys?" he asked.

"This, Dad, this," Ryan told him as he opened his hand and held a little box out to his father.

The pills.

"When we're in the car," Mr. Bartlett replied in a low voice, "a little more private, okay?"

They both nodded.

The "car," complete with a driver, was one provided for them by a bigwig at the agency's headquarters.

"A limousine!" Ryan exclaimed.

"What'll I do with my bike?" Chad asked.

"Somebody will bring it home to us later," Mr. Bartlett told him.

"I've gotta let a stranger take care of my bike?"

He shrugged his shoulders when the two of them looked at him with mock sternness.

"All right already," he said.

Once inside, in the back seat, with the glass partition rolled up, Andrew Bartlett told his sons, "It's what we're *supposed* to do. Rather than reveal secrets, or anything like that, we're supposed to crunch down on one of those, and—."

"Suicide, Dad," Ryan protested. "That's suicide."

"I know. That's why I've never taken any of the capsules with me."

"You haven't?" Chad said, relieved.

"I've thrown away the rest, and keep only those in the safe-deposit box, as a reminder."

"But . . . but—," Ryan started to ask, but nervous about the question.

"Out with it," his father urged.

"Isn't that disobeying your superiors?"

"Of course it is. But, Ryan, there are times in life when we *do* have to choose between God and Man. That's what it's all about, you know."

Ryan nodded.

"I love you," he said exactly one second before Chad said the same thing.

"And I love you guys more than I can say."

They leaned over, the three of them, and hugged one another.

That evening, Ryan managed to do some homework on his computer. Afterwards he joined his father and his brother for one of Miss Stephenson's delicious dinners.

They stayed up very late that night, talking over the past few days and praying. When they finally went upstairs to bed, all three of them were just about asleep on their feet.

Ryan forgot to turn the computer off. It remained on all night.

There was a sudden storm not long after midnight, which caused a brief power outage, wiping a message off the monitor, a message Ryan would never get to see.

IT'S NOT OVER. WE KNOW, WHO YOU ARE. BELIEVE THAT WE'LL TRY AGAIN. YES, BELIEVE THAT. OUR REVOLUTION CAN'T BE STOPPED.

AND WE'LL FIND YOU. YOU WON'T ESCAPE. THERE WILL BE NO WARNING NEXT TIME.

THINK ABOUT THAT. THINK ABOUT IT A GREAT DEAL.

ESPECIALLY AT NIGHT . . . WHEN YOU'RE ALONE.

DON'T MISS THESE OTHER BARTLETT BROTHER ADVENTURES:

Terror Cruise
The Bartlett family embarks on a Caribbean cruise that is supposed to be a time of rest and relaxation, but instead becomes a journey into terror. (ISBN 0–8499–3302–1)

The Frankenstein Project
While visiting a friend in the hospital, Ryan and Chad Bartlett come face to face with secret scientific experiments and mysterious children. (ISBN 0–8499–3303–X, available September 1991)

Forbidden River
The brothers find themselves in the midst of an international conflict when their father, who is a U. S. diplomat, is kidnapped by drug lords in South America. (ISBN 0–8499–3304–8, available September 1991)